BUILDING ROMANCE

ROMANCES IN THE BUILDING SERIES
BOOK 3

S.E. ROSE

CHAPTER ONE

Cam

"Why is it so hard to find good dick?" Drew asks with exasperation as he strolls into my café as if he owns the place.

I glance up at him from where I'm making sourdough bread and fight a smirk.

"Uh, is that a trick question?" I ask, looking around to ensure another customer hasn't snuck in here even though I know I'm alone.

"Well, let me tell you about my latest text from this guy," he sighs and sits down at my counter. He starts to prattle on about a conversation he's having on a dating app, while I continue my work.

The feeling of the dough beneath my fingers is as familiar as the air I breathe. It's soothing. My senses are filled to the brim. The sourdough beneath my fingers, the smell of the chocolate chip muffins in the oven, the sounds of Drew's voice as he speaks, the taste on my tongue of the cookie I just sampled a minute ago, and the sight of Drew waving his hands animatedly as he speaks. I glance down at my dough. It's nearly ready to proof.

Between school and bakery jobs, I've worked for a solid decade toward a goal. And last week, that goal was achieved when I opened my very own bakery. I can hardly believe it. I feel like pinching myself again just to prove that all of this is real.

When my former boss, Phyllis, decided to retire a few months ago, she offered to sell her business to me. The landlord for the property likes having a café here and agreed to sign the lease with me. I snagged a small business loan, and just like that, everything fell into place.

Well, nearly everything. I glare at the empty building down the street. A large banner sign hangs over the front door.

"McDowell's Coming Soon"

I grimace. I've worked so hard and I felt like I nearly had it all figured out. I was going to be that quintessential success story. I *was*.

"Turn that frown upside down," Drew says, breaking my train of thought. Regardless of how discouraged I feel right now, the thought that my closest friend is sitting in *my* café does make me smile a little.

"That's better. The usual, by the way," Drew states as he swivels in the barstool and types furiously on his phone without looking up at me, clearly responding to this man he just ranted about for the last five minutes. "I am so over this new guy. I swear he's the most annoying human ever born."

I raise an eyebrow at my best friend. Drew had been in a serious relationship until a few months ago. Drew was dating an Italian man who finished his graduate degree and went back to Italy. He pretends it's no big deal, but I know he's still heartbroken.

And now, well, he's swiping right on one-night stands. I

hate seeing him like this. I know deep down, he wants a serious relationship. Hell, the man reads more romance books than I do.

"So, no second date?" I ask as I make his coffee and pull out an orange cinnamon roll, something I added to the bakery menu when I reopened as Cam's Café. I set the roll on a plate and push it toward him.

He finally glances up at me. "Hell no. He wore a paisley shirt, Cam. The entire shirt was paisley," he grimaces.

I giggle as I finish making his caramel latte with mocha cold foam. The man has a new fancy drink order monthly and this is his new usual drink, at least for the next two weeks.

"I mean, there are worse offenses," I state with a knowing look.

"True. That guy you went out with a few weeks ago wore cargo shorts. It's freaking winter practically and...cargo shorts. Just no," he says. "Thank God I was there to rescue you."

"I'll cheers to that," I say as I clink my coffee mug with his after I set it down. I wouldn't say I've given up on love, but it's definitely taken a back seat while I've been getting my café up and running.

"Morning," my new employee, Adriana, says as she walks through the front door. She's a young college student, but she worked as a barista in high school and only lives a few blocks away. So far, she's been great. I kept Amber, my baking assistant, on my team. She's worked here with me for years. She's a few years older than me and a single mom. And then there's Hugh. He's older and takes care of stocking my shelves, cleaning, repairs, and basically anything I ask him to do. It's a small team, but a good one.

"Morning," Drew and I say in unison.

"Banana bread still in the oven?" she asks as she walks back toward the kitchen.

"Yep, should be done in about five minutes," I answer.

She nods and I watch as she disappears into the back.

"How's that working out?" Drew asks, nodding toward the door.

I shrug. "So far, so good," I state as I walk back into my kitchen and slide the dough I was kneading into my warming oven.

I wash my hands and step back out to find Drew smiling at his phone.

"Dick pic?" I ask with a smirk.

He glances up at me and rolls his eyes. "Nope," he says as he sips his coffee.

"Gonna share with the class?" I ask.

"Nope," he replies.

"You are exasperating," I groan while wiping down my marble counter.

"I know, but that's why you love me. Also, you're grumpy. You need to get laid," he says with a laugh as he gets up and places his glass in a bin for dirty dishes. I glare at him, but I can't even be mad because he's right. "Toodeloo. I'm off for a mani. These nails are ragged as fuck," he states with a wave.

"You home for dinner?" I call out as he opens the door.

"Yeah." He pauses. "Chinese?"

I tilt my head as I contemplate our food options. "Yeah. Golden Palace?" I suggest.

"Exactly. The usual?" he asks.

I nod.

"Oh, can you look again for my grandmother's saltshaker?" I ask. Last week, my grandmother's saltshaker that she got at the 1964 World's Fair in New York went missing. I don't know if it's because the salt and pepper shakers are shaped like telephones or that they are historic or because they remind me of cooking in her kitchen with her, but I love them. And I'm heartbroken to be missing one. I don't know why, but I always use that stupid saltshaker and I feel like it's my good luck charm.

"Yeah. I'll look again," he says giving me an encouraging smile. He's already scoured the kitchen for it. As much as he drives me nuts, he's a good guy.

He waves as he exits the café and heads down the street to the nail salon. He loves getting his nails done. The man always has them buffed, no polish. He actually got our giant, former-football-player neighbor, Hutch, to go with him a few months ago after a year of nagging. Now, the two have mani-pedi days once a month. I haven't had time to go. I glance at my nails that desperately need shaping. I really ought to make time to take better care of myself. Hell, I need time for anything...like finding a guy. Drew is right. I need some dick.

———

I lie in my bed and stare at my phone, willing it to vibrate with an incoming message.

Nothing. Damn it. What the hell is Max doing? He always replies right away.

Last year, I started chatting with this man on a dating app where there are no photos. Drew suggested it. I'm always drawn to a certain type of man based on looks and it has never once worked out well. So, begrudgingly, I took his advice. Three days later, I started talking to a man named Max. We eventually decided we should just be friends after he admitted to hating my absolute favorite sports team and also scoffed at the fact that I love reading romance novels. I told him we were incompatible. He sent twelve laughing emojis...TWELVE. And then I rage ignored him for two days. But after he sent me an e-gift card to my favorite spa to an email I shared with him, I eventually forgave him and we've been talking nonstop since then. I still swear we are not compatible, but that hasn't stopped us from being friends.

I grab my e-reader and try to distract myself with my latest read. It's an enemies to lovers. There's just something about the trope that I love. But I also think it's completely unrealistic. Or I did, until my friend Gray ended up with his now girlfriend, Roxy. They both live here in my apartment building. Roxy owns a romance bookstore on the first floor of the building. And at first, they hated each other. But now, it's like a flip switched and all that anger turned into off-the-charts passion. They actually make me a little sick with how sweet they are to each other. And then Kasen, my other friend, who happens to be a scary-looking ex-military guy who barely speaks, somehow landed a sweet and happy woman who is his exact opposite.

My phone vibrates on my nightstand and I toss the e-reader onto the bed and glance over to see a notification. Max has texted me.

Max: I thought your business was doing great. No?

I had told him I was worried about a competitor moving in near my café.

When Max and I started talking, we had decided to not discuss anything that would be too personal. No names of people we know. I honestly wonder if Max is his real name. I use my middle name, Eliza, on the app. No saying where we worked or what industry. Nothing that would make us easily identifiable. We just wanted to get to know each other without the desire to internet stalk.

For reasons that I really haven't considered, we've kept up this weird charade where we talk about life but with no identifiers. So he knows I just bought a business and I have a store, but he has no idea that it's a café. I know his family owns a business and he works for it. But I couldn't tell you what he does or what the business is.

It's the absolute strangest relationship I've ever had, yet, there's something very liberating about it. I can complain about anything I want and there is zero judgment. I love Drew, but my bestie is a judgy-judgerkins.

Me: I mean, it is for now.

Max: Get the local community behind you. Locals have a way of making or breaking a business.

Me: Says the businessman.

I can't help wondering what kind of business his family owns, but I sort of like daydreaming about it. In my mind, they own a local car mechanic shop or a flower shop or something. He did mention once that whatever the family owns has been in operation since his great-grandparents, which I think is pretty cool. I told him I hoped my store would be run by my great-grandchildren someday.

Max: You need to play offensive. I'll send you a list of books you should read.

Me: (eye-rolling emoji)

Max: I'm serious.

Me: OK, Professor Max.

Max: I sort of like that. (questioning emoji)

Me: On that note, I'm going to bed.

Max: Goodnight, my little entrepreneur.

Me: Goodnight, Professor Max.

I toss my phone on my nightstand and grab my e-reader. I look at the links Max has texted and download two of the books he recommends. I mean, it can't hurt to learn. And if it means I find a way to crush McDowell's, then it'll be worth it.

CHAPTER TWO

Fletch

Dalton and Spencer stare at me as if I'm an idiot child that just won the spelling bee. To be fair, they often stare at me like this, and I suppose I've brought it upon myself.

"Dad, you can't be serious," Spencer says not breaking eye contact with me.

I'm both pissed off and also shocked. My father has just announced that he's decided to put me in charge of our latest store opening. Me. Am I capable? Yes. Am I an expected choice? Hell, yes.

Being the youngest of three brothers, the first two being very type A, makes me the family fuckup. It probably doesn't help that I spent most of my teens and twenties doing exactly that...fucking up. I slept with way too many women; I jaunted off to places like Ibiza on the family jet whenever I felt like attending a rave; and then there was the time I maybe dropped forty thousand on renting a private island for all of my frat brothers and me for spring break. That last one made the news and not in a good way.

So, yes, I've spent the last six-plus years trying to redeem myself, but I've dug such a deep hole, I'm not sure any of my family take me seriously...until now.

I turn to look at our dad. Edward McDowell is an icon in the coffee world. He runs one of the largest coffee and café companies not just in our country but in approximately ten other countries. He normally has an entire division of the company that works on finding real estate, acquiring real estate, and then building the café. So, why he wants me to lead that team for our latest acquisition, I haven't a clue.

"Are you serious?" I ask, reiterating Spencer's question.

"Yes." His single word echoes around his office. Dalton smirks at me and I glare back at him. Dalton is the oldest. He's forty, divorced with one kid, a little boy named Timothy. I love his son. He's the coolest kid I know. Dalton can be a bit of an asshole. He's in line to take over the family company. I both love and hate him. He's brilliant, but unforgiving and stubborn as hell.

"Dad, we have a division that handles that," Spencer points out. Spencer is the middle child. He likes things neat and orderly. He's only three years older than me, but he might as well be one hundred. He takes life way too seriously. Where I was the wild party child, he was the closet nerd. He spent his childhood locked in the family library and participating in every club and sport at the elite private academy we attended. He's never been married and seldom dates. He does hook up with plenty of women, but nothing serious. To be fair, he had a very serious girlfriend who slept with what used to be his best friend, and his best friend's old brother, and half of his soccer team. That was in college, and the man has never been the same.

"Spencer, I've made my decision. There will not be a

discussion. Louis is taking a leave of absence to be home with his wife while she goes through chemotherapy, and I'm assigning Fletcher to lead them," he says and steeples his fingers. That's Dad's tell that the conversation is over. Fucking fantastic.

———

I look up at the building as I stand on the sidewalk. The operations team has already signed a lease for the property, so at least I don't have to find us a location. But we haven't started any of the construction yet. I unlock the door and walk inside.

And, I immediately regret that decision. This place is a total dump. What the hell were they thinking? They want to open in less than four months. There's no fucking way.

I pull my phone out and call Dalton.

"This is a mess. Who am I blaming?" I ask him as I walk through the space. The building is stripped on the interior but there are boxes and construction supplies everywhere. No one is working, and from the look of it, we need the general contractor to have a crew here around the clock.

"Rich's team chose the location. And Frank's team bid out the contract. Why? What's wrong with it? Dad said it's a great location," Dalton asks.

"Great? Has he even come to see it?" I inquire. It's unusual for us to open a store in this city. We have our flagship store downtown and approximately ten others in the greater metro area. But real estate in this neighborhood seldom comes on the market. I can understand the draw. It's a nice street, residential, and that means it's full of customers that will drink our coffee and eat our baked goods.

"Nope. That's your job, big guy. Best of luck," Dalton says

and I know that fucker is smirking. He is enjoying each and every moment of this.

"Fuck you. This place is a shithole. There's no way we can have it ready in four months," I protest.

"Make it happen, baby boy," Dalton says, using the obnoxious nickname my mom has used for me, since birth.

"I should have taken that job offer to work in the food television industry. At least I'd be in a climate-controlled office right now," I state as I unbutton my shirt and loosen my tie. The building's air system is clearly not operable and it's an unusually warm winter day.

"Guess so. Have fun, fucker. Dad picked that location for the neighborhood, not the building. You have your work cut out for you," he says as he disconnects.

I run a hand through my hair and sit down on a box.

I pull out my phone and call the only person besides my brothers that I trust. My grandmother. I love my parents but they are delusional. And the few friends I have left after leaving the party scene have zero idea about this shit and could care less. Now, I just want to prove to my father that I can do this. Maybe, if I can make this work, he'll trust me to do what I really want to do.

I've pitched him the idea to sponsor some reality food competition shows. We could put the winning baked goods in the stores. I love the idea of finding raw talent. My brief stint working with a professional baker made me appreciate all the small bakery businesses out there with incredible pastry chefs that never get enough clout. And I could merge what I want to do with the family business. But he doesn't see the merit of the idea.

The phone rings and she answers.

"Fletch, my darling, how are you?" she answers in her weathered voice that instantly soothes me.

"I'm sitting in our new location on Hearts Lane," I say,

because I don't have the heart to tell her it needs more work than I think we have time to complete. My grandparents have long ago turned the business over to Dad, but they still deeply care about it and run most of our charity work.

"Oh? I heard Eddie put you in charge. That's so exciting. You get to put your very own spin on it," she encourages. She's not wrong. I do. But my heart's not really in Hearts Lane.

"I suppose," I agree.

"Go on any dates lately?" she asks.

I roll my eyes. Gran Hattie, or Gran Ha as we affectionately call her, is determined that all three of us boys will get married and give her great-grandbabies. Dad's younger brother, Jasper, married an awesome man named Giddeon. I love them dearly, but they are more interested in spending time at their Cape Cod beach house, gardening, and going to the local pub for trivia night. Neither has ever been interested in our family business.

"Nope. Pretty busy, Gran Ha," I say, using her nickname that Dalton created when he was two and couldn't pronounce her name.

"You need to enjoy life a little. I'm proud of you for working hard lately, but all work and no play makes Jack a dull boy," she states.

"I'll work on that," I say, attempting to appease her.

I'm quiet for a bit and it's as if she senses my unease.

"What's really wrong with my off-the-record favorite grandson?" she asks. I smile. I know I'm her favorite. We've had a connection since I was a baby.

"It's just...overwhelming. What if I fuck this up?" I admit.

"What if you mess it up?" she corrects me.

"Yeah, that," I say as I roll my eyes again.

"Well, you figure out how to fix it. You're a smart boy. Even when you messed up as a kid, you always figured out a way to make it right," she points out. I did. And damn, fixing my fuckups were often ten times harder than planning them.

"What would you do?" I ask her.

She pauses and I know she's considering it. "You need to win over the neighborhood and get them excited. And you need to get our team to meet with the general contractor. Maybe we need to hire a different one if you aren't pleased with their work. Is that the issue?"

She's so fucking smart.

"Yep. Place is a mess," I admit.

"I figured so. I know the building. It's right by Al's place," she says.

Al O'Brien. He's played poker with my grandfather for years. Maybe I should pay him a visit.

"Yes, it is."

"You there now?" she asks.

"I am." I stand and dust off my pants.

"You should go visit him. I'm sure he'd love to see you," she suggests.

"I'll do that. Thanks, Gran Ha," I say.

"Love you, Fletch," she says.

"Love you, too," I reply as we hang up and I walk out onto the street.

I walk down the block to one-eleven Hearts Lane. I glance across the street and see a small café, but it's not the competing business that draws my attention, it's the mess of red hair atop the most beautiful face I've ever seen. The woman doesn't see me. She's busy making a coffee drink and talking to a man at the counter. I stand transfixed for a minute, unable to turn away.

"Checking out your competition?"

I turn and see Al. Smiling, I hug him, patting his back before pulling away.

"How are you?" I ask as I stand back and look at him.

He's aged, but he still looks like the same kind man I remember from my childhood.

"You know, getting old," he answers with a laugh.

"Well, you look the same to me," I reply. And I'm not lying. The man hasn't changed a bit in nearly twenty-five years. My brothers say his hair was more brown when we were little, but I only remember him from the time I was in first grade. That's when Gran Ha would pick me up after school three days a week so we could work on my reading. I had dyslexia and she had a degree in special education. And as a treat, I got to sit in on my grandfather's poker game on Thursday nights. Al was always my favorite of his friends.

"Guess all the walking keeps me young." He points to a trail at the end of the street. There's a park there and it looks inviting. "Care to join me?"

I shrug. "Why not?" I say as we begin to walk.

"So tell me, what is the great Fletcher McDowell up to these days?" he asks.

I chuckle and fill him in as we walk along a river down to a pond. By the time we make it back to the street, I'm feeling better. Al didn't say much, just listened, and I think that's what I needed, someone who is willing to listen to me, no judging, just listen.

"No ladies in your life?" Al asks as I see him to the door of his apartment building that he owns.

"Nope," I reply, glancing over at the café to see the redhead rolling some dough on a marble counter. She tucks a stray hair behind her ear and I get the overwhelming urge to want to touch that hair. I quickly look away. I'm being crazy.

Al follows my gaze. "That's Cam. She just bought the place recently. It's the neighborhood favorite." He leans forward. "I'm on Team Cam's Café, by the way."

I laugh. "Is that so?"

He nods. "I love your family, but that little café has so

many memories for me. Edith loved it." He gives me a sad smile as he says his late wife's name.

"I remember. Didn't Phyllis own it?" I ask, remembering the owner's name.

"She did. She just retired a few weeks ago," he explains.

"Oh." I had figured Phyllis would retire soon and close shop, but it appears my competition is remaining. Al raises a good point. It's a neighborhood hot spot. I need to figure out a way to make us different from this café. And that means, I need to scope it out.

"Well, I need to get back to the office," I say as I shake his hand.

"Good luck, kid. I think you're going to need it," he calls out with a smile as he walks inside his building.

I smirk. "I don't think I will. The best part of being underestimated is that no one sees you coming," I murmur to myself. I look back over at the woman. "Prepare to go down, Cam's Café."

CHAPTER THREE

Cam

It's pouring outside and I watch as a hooded man walks briskly across the street and opens the door. He shakes his coat a little and pulls the hood back slightly. And hot damn. He is very attractive. He's tall and has dark hair and pale blue eyes. He has thick dark lashes that would make any woman jealous. He's muscular but not in a Hutch or a Kasen way. Why my two friends feel the need to constantly pump iron at the gym is beyond me. My brain momentarily short-circuits and I imagine this mystery man lifting me up and slamming me into a wall as he devours my mouth.

Pull it together! I chastise myself.

"What can I get you?" I ask.

His hair is a little wet and has a slight curl to it. He pushes it back off his forehead and glances up at the menu behind me.

"I'll have a medium salted caramel pistachio latte," he

orders. His voice is...well, I want to ask if he narrates spicy romance books because if he doesn't, he should.

"Sure thing," I reply as I get to work making it.

I go to say something to him about his audiobook-worthy voice, but the door swings open again and a very drenched Hutch walks inside. He shakes his head like a dog, droplets of water splattering everywhere.

"Hutch!" I admonish.

"For the love of..." he groans and grabs my mop from around the door to the kitchen. He wipes up the water and places it back.

Raspy-deep-voice mystery man watches him. His gaze flickering between us.

"My lady," Hutch says, bowing slightly.

I roll my eyes. "Usual?" I ask as I hand my new customer his drink. Hutch nods.

"Any luck finding that saltshaker that went missing?" Hutch asks.

I shake my head. My lucky saltshaker has been missing for a week now.

"Bummer," he replies.

I glance back over at the mystery man. My inner twentysomething-year-old Cam desperately wants to write my number on the cup I've handed this man. But somehow, I muster all my maturity and refrain.

"Here you are. Anything else?" I ask as I ring him up.

He shakes his head and taps his card on the reader.

"Thanks," he mutters as he turns and takes a seat by the window, pulling out his phone and typing away.

With a shrug, I turn my attention back to Hutch.

"So, any luck today?" I ask, nodding toward the park.

"Nope," he sighs and grabs a napkin, wiping the water off his face.

The door swings open again and Jocelyn, who works at

the bookstore across the road, walks inside. She sets her umbrella by the door.

"I didn't know we had a monsoon season so late in the year," she grumbles.

Hutch chuckles. "What? You want that to be snow? We'd be stuck inside for days."

"Still, I'd love to see the sun. It's been like four straight days of this," she protests as she motions outside.

"Fair. I hear the day after tomorrow is supposed to be nice," he says. He's looking at her intently and I just know they have a crush on each other. I wish they'd just hook up already.

"I hope so," she answers before turning to me. "Can I get two of the daily specials?" she asks.

"Sure thing," I reply as I set Hutch's coffee down.

My gaze darts to the mystery man and I find him watching me. I freeze for a millisecond and then give him a smile and pretend that I'm not completely disarmed by him.

Jocelyn looks over her shoulder and then leans over the counter.

"Uh, who is bachelor number one?" she whispers.

Hutch leans over her. And I mean that literally. He is so tall and she is so short that he leans all the way over her.

"What are we whispering about, ladies? You know I love gossip almost as much as Drew," he says in a low voice.

Jocelyn giggles and elbows him and then he wraps an arm around her middle and lifts her from the floor as if she's a feather.

"Cut it out," she laughs.

He sets her down. "But seriously, what's the tea?"

My eyes flick back over to the mystery man. He stands and pulls his hood back up and walks out into the now lessening rain.

"Holy shitballs!" Hutch says loudly.

Jocelyn slaps her hand over his mouth and he bites her finger.

"Ewww! Gross," she mutters as she pulls her hand away.

"What?" I ask, finishing Jocelyn's drinks and setting them on the counter.

"You don't know who that is?" he asks as he looks at me.

I shake my head, frowning as I try to place the man.

"That," he starts and points toward the door, "is Fletcher McDowell."

I grip the counter because I feel woozy.

There's no way. Fletcher has to be a troll. Anyone related to the McDowells must be ugly because that would make sense. They are literally trying to put me out of business with their new shop across the street. Fletcher most certainly cannot be that attractive. Damn it! I just started developing a crush on my mortal enemy.

"And he just left?" Roxy asks. Roxy, my neighbor who owns the bookstore directly across the street, is waiting on her order and we are gossiping about Fletcher McDowell's visit a few days ago.

"Yep. He's a total creeper," I state as I add the milk to the lattes she ordered for her and Jocelyn. Those two have become my best customers and they always send their customers over to me.

"What are we going to do?" she questions while picking at a lavender, lemon, blueberry glazed muffin.

"I think I need everyone's advice," I declare as I hand her the drinks. And by everyone, I mean my whole building. Above Roxy's bookstore are five more floors of apartments, and their inhabitants have become my closest friends.

"We'll figure something out," she says.

"Max suggested some books to read," I state as I wipe my counter.

She gives me a pointed look. "You're still talking with him. Why don't you two just go out? It's been months."

I shrug. "I don't think it'd work out, and plus, I'd hate to lose him as a friend. He's a jackass about certain things, but he's a good guy and a great listener."

She shakes her head at me as she takes the drinks and the bag of muffins with her. She turns her head when she's at the door. "Don't forget to have a little fun. You've made this place your whole life. Make sure to still enjoy the other parts of your life."

She's not wrong. I've been putting all my energy into this. It's hard work and I'm trying to figure it all out. My older brother, Winston, and my parents have always babied me. This place was a way to prove to them that I'm capable all on my own. But I haven't left time for anything other than our apartment building's weekly happy hours and an occasional ladies' night at my neighbors' apartment. So I guess if socializing with women forty years older than me is considered an extracurricular, then I'm living large.

I sigh. Even my oldest neighbors, Margie and Cornelia, date.

"See you later," Roxy calls out as she opens the door and I watch her cross the street.

"Fuck," I mutter. I forgot to change my menu by the front door. I like to add new specials every week. I go in the back and print out the latest list of specialty items.

Grabbing the keys to the small glass cabinet that the menus hang in by the door, I go and unlock it. I notice movement to my right. Out of the corner of my eye, I see it's none other than Fletcher McDowell in the flesh. He's wearing a suit today and is definitely not here incognito.

"Spying again?" I ask as I change the menu by the door. I don't bother looking up at him.

I can tell he has stopped walking based on the silence. I finish hanging the menu and glance over and our gazes lock. I glare at him.

Then for reasons that escape me, I decide to ignore him and walk inside and around my counter. He follows me. I start placing baked goods on the counter.

"You want to take these and try to recreate them?" He doesn't move. "No? Oh, maybe you want my latte recipes?" I walk over to the wall and point to the ingredients under each item.

This time he does move. In three giant strides, he steps in front of me. My eyes stay locked on his, although now my head has to tip up to see him.

I jut my chin out defiantly.

"I'd like to make you an offer," he states.

Now, I'm aware of all those redhead cliches. The ones that say we have a fiery temper. And I absolutely hate following the stereotype. And I hate this man for making me. But his words turn me into a raging person that may resemble a trapped lion.

"An offer of what?" I say through gritted teeth.

"I'd like to buy your café," he says in that deep, raspy voice. Only now, I find it grating instead of sexy. Fuck him.

"It's. Not. For. Sale," I manage. My temper is barely staying in check. I'm three seconds away from a total epic meltdown that would rival the Hulk.

"Everything is for sale," he says and then adds, "For the right price."

"That's it. Get out. Get the fuck out," I blurt out, immediately regretting letting this asshat push me to lose my cool.

He raises one eyebrow, as if to say he didn't think I had it in me, and then he raises one hand in one of those "calm down" motions.

"The offer will stay on the table for thirty days. But know that I have enough money to put you out of business even if I don't buy your café."

I hate that his words are true. I hate Fletcher McDowell.

I point to the door.

"You want a war, Mr. McDowell?" I raise an eyebrow to mirror him. "You got one. This neighborhood is loyal and no amount of dirty money will change that. So best of luck."

His lips twitch slightly. Is this motherfucker laughing at me?

I point to the door again and this time he turns and leaves without looking back.

I shake a little when the door closes. I need a plan and I need one now.

I text Max.

Me: How do you take down a competitor?

Max: Now we're talking.

Me: I'm serious.

Max: Friends close, enemies closer.

Me: Yeah, yeah. I just...ugh!

Max: Did you read the books I suggested?

Me: I skimmed them.

Max: So, how are you going to find the chink in the armor?

Me: I need to think about it, but I was hoping you had a brilliant idea.

Max: Well, I still think you should keep your enemy close, but if you are completely opposed to that, then figure out a way you can outsmart them and then rebrand yourself in a way they don't see coming.

Me: (thinking emoji) Not a bad idea.

Max: (smart emoji)
Me: (eye-rolling emoji)

CHAPTER FOUR

Fletch

I finish my whiskey and set the glass on my brother's island.

"She had the audacity to ask if I wanted a war? Like, what the fuck?" I state angrily. I was trying to do the right thing by buying her out. Well, it'd also make my life easier, but that's beside the point. If I could buy her café, I could close it down and get rid of our competition. We would become the new neighborhood hot spot. And I could finally prove to my family that I'm not some fuckup playboy any longer. But now, this fiery pain-in-my-ass woman is trying to win a war against me. She's a thorn in my side and I'm going to have to deal with her the hard way.

"So, what's the plan?" Spencer asks as he pours me another two fingers of whiskey.

"Not sure. I either need to work with our marketing team to come up with some way to convert the neighborhood into loving us more, or I need to find something that will make her cave," I contemplate aloud.

"Well, cheers to taking down the competition," Spencer says as he clinks his glass against mine.

"I have this sneaking suspicion she is going to be the death of me," I mutter remembering how she brushed that red hair out of her face when she was trying to put me in my place. The fact that I find her attractive only makes me angrier. It's like her beauty is mocking me, trying to play on my past playboy ways. I'm not that person any longer and I will prove it one way or another.

"How is it going over there?" Spencer asks as he adjusts his glasses and leans back against his counter. I look around his kitchen. It is so Spencer. Everything is black and white and clean. There's not a single thing out on the counter aside from the glasses and whiskey bottle. I, on the other hand, have all my small appliances sitting out on mine and likely day-old glasses and plates in my sink. I gave my housekeeper the week off and I'm regretting not taking her up on the offer to get her fill-in to come by and clean for me.

"It's not going. I'm going to have to crack some skulls. There was zero work happening when I went over yesterday. I think Jason has all his subs over at a worksite downtown. Things will be changing this week or his ass is getting fired," I grumble.

"That's the spirit. I'd also encourage you to go talk with Georgia. She can start work on a marketing plan now to counteract what is happening. I know she already had some things planned but she should know that our competition is going to be a pain for us," Spencer points out. He's right. Damn, this is tough. I've got so many teams to manage. I finish my drink and hop off the stool I'm sitting on as I grab my coat from Spencer's hall closet.

"I got stuff to do. We're still going to the lake this weekend, yeah?" I ask, changing the topic because a weekend away at the lake seems like a safer thing to fixate on than my gorgeous rival.

He nods. "Yeah. I had the staff prep the house for winter. We're supposed to start getting some weather," he says.

"Great. See you later," I say as I head downstairs while deep in thought. Maybe I should talk to Al. I need to get more intel on Camryn Tanner. I've searched her up online. She's two years younger than me. She's from the area, although she apparently spent some of her childhood living in a different city. She's got one older brother. Her parents are still together and she has lots of photos with some guy name Drew Whiteford. She studied culinary arts in college. And she worked at a few restaurants before landing a job at the café she now owns. The café has some great reviews.

Nothing stands out that feels like a chink in her armor. But that isn't stopping me from looking for that one small thing that can help me bring her down. Everyone has a price, some people just need to be nudged in order to accept it. And that stubborn woman definitely seems like the type that needs a nudge.

———

"Have you considered sponsoring a local bakery yet for this year's City Bake-Off competition?" Dalton asks.

We're sitting in our conference room going over upcoming items. Until I officially joined my brothers and father several years ago at the helm of our company, I didn't even know they had weekly meetings. Shit, there was a lot that I didn't know.

"No," Spencer states. "I wish we could enter it."

My father sighs. "The competition isn't about giant companies, Spence. It's a chance to advertise for us. But we have to sponsor a contestant. Bridget has already reached out to inquire about it. It'll be televised again this year, so there are commercial spots. Our marketing team is keen on us working with a local bakery. Any ideas?"

My father looks around the table. Georgia, our marketing lead, leans forward.

"What about that little bakery by the site for the new store?" she asks.

Everyone's heads turn to me. "Cam's?" I ask as I feel the color draining from my face. She has to be kidding me. I don't want to work with Cam. I don't want to be anywhere near her. I need to keep her far away, not closer. Although, I know I should keep my enemies close. But I'm not about to take my own advice.

"Yeah, Fletch. How about Cam's?" Dalton asks, that patented smirk fighting to emerge. God, my brother is such an ass.

Georgia looks between us with a raised eyebrow. "You know what they say, right?" Everyone glances her way. "Keep your friends close and your enemies closer." Of course, she'd fucking say that.

"But why would we want to promote a competitor?" I ask, questioning her sanity.

"Because, our standard sponsorship contract has always included a provision that gives us final say in the company's decisions per the competition," she says nonchalantly as if I'm a giant idiot.

"And?" I ask. "Who cares if we tell her to make cupcakes instead of cookies for the final round?"

She smirks. "You're missing the trees through the forest. We can sabotage her if we want. We could have her make something horrible. Or change something at the last minute. It airs on television. The judges all say it's no good and voilà. Competition gone."

I lean back in my chair. Well, shit. Georgia raises an excellent point.

Sabotage my competitor. Yeah, I could do that.

"Who's going to approach her?" I ask.

"You," my father states not leaving a second for discussion.

I hold up my hand. "There's no way she'll agree to it, then. We've already had an...encounter," I state.

"So what? She'll want to do this. There's no way she gets more exposure than with this show," my father says. He has a point. This is the biggest baked goods competition in our area. Any bakery or café worth their weight in gold would want to compete, to have an opportunity to prove themselves. Plus, the winner gets a shit ton of money and free advertising. And I know Cam won't be able to pass that opportunity up.

"Fine. But if she doesn't bite with my pitch, then one of you will need to step in," I muse as I contemplate how I'll pitch this to her. One misstep and Cam's fuse is likely to explode.

"Great. That's settled. Let's move on to the issue we are having with the McDowell's in Kensington," my father says as he pulls up a slide from his laptop and launches into a dipping sales situation with one of our British stores.

But my head is still stuck on Cam's Café, or Cam if I'm being honest with myself. How am I going to get her to agree? She all but threw down a gauntlet when we last spoke. However, it's not her words that burned their imprint on my brain, it was the way her messy hair fell on her cheek and the way her arms pushed up her chest when she crossed them in defiance. She's the type of woman who's naturally beautiful and yet Cam Tanner doesn't seem to care at all what I think about her beauty. She's fixated on winning, on being the best. And honestly, that is a million times hotter than anything about her physically. It's dangerous. I can't be attracted to the enemy. I may have put my player ways aside when I came to work here, but that doesn't mean I don't find women attractive. I've been stuck in a hookup-buddy loop for three years. Do I want more? Maybe.

There's just one thing I can't want. Camryn Tanner.

CHAPTER FIVE

Cam

"He did not!" Drew exclaims as he sets his cocktail down on the bar.

It's Thursday night, which means it's happy hour on the rooftop deck of my apartment building. Al, the owner, always throws one each week and sometimes other days for special occasions. Everyone is here, and after a discussion of where my saltshaker might have gone, we've turned the conversation to McDowell's.

"He did," I grumble as Al sets down an extra-dirty martini with five blue-cheese-stuffed olives. He slides it toward me. I down it and start eating the olives.

"Whoa, slow down there. We can figure this out," Bray says as he adjusts Ava on his lap.

"There is a belted kingfisher in the park!" Troy exclaims as he throws open the door and looks around wildly, a pair of binoculars in his hand.

Everyone stops talking and gives him a curious look. Troy

and his wife, Jessa, are the building's official parents. They also take care of all the plumbing, electric, construction, and administrative work for Al. I guess I knew Troy liked birds. He does have an African gray parrot named Rocky. And I do see him on occasion in the park watching birds. But I've never seen him going crazy about a bird.

"I'm sorry, a what?" Carly asks as she leans on the counter next to Bray.

"Mom, he said a—" Ava starts but Carly holds up a hand.

"I heard him, little nugget. But I don't know what that is," she explains.

Ava turns to Troy. "Mr. Troy, is that a special bird or something?"

He nods enthusiastically and takes the camera hanging around his chest off, turning it around to show everyone the screen. Like the good found family we are, we all gather in a circle and "ooh" and "ahh" about a small bird.

"That makes over one hundred birds this year," Jessa says as she squeezes her husband's shoulder.

"It does. A great birding year," he says proudly.

"Troy, how did I not know you were such a bird enthusiast?" Roxy asks as Gray pulls her back against him.

He shrugs. "It's not a big deal. A man has to have a hobby. I can't be all wires and pipes all the time," he says.

Drew chokes on his drink. "Yeah, definitely not all pipes all the time."

I roll my eyes at my bestie.

"What'd I miss?" Troy asks as Al hands him his usual boring beer.

"Well, we're figuring out how to derail the opening of the McDowell's down the street," Al explains.

Roxy turns to Kasen who is sitting at the bar with Hutch and Bray. "Can't you, like, do some high-tech cyber thing and ruin the store?"

"No," Kasen grunts.

"Oh, come on," she urges and elbows Piper, Kasen's girl-friend. "He can, right?"

Piper shrugs. "Beats me."

"That would be illegal," Kasen says as he raises an eyebrow in my direction. He's the strong and silent type, but I'm pretty sure he could kill me with his bare hands if he was so inclined.

"Right," I mumble.

"How about the winter festival? It's coming up soon. We could have a huge marketing campaign here in the neighbor-hood. I mean, Al knows everyone, right, Al?" Margie suggests and Cornelia nods in agreement. The grandmothers of our building have spoken. And it's not a terrible plan, but how is one strong showing at a booth at a festival going to change anything. Everyone here already knows about the café. I need new customers.

"She'll be there, but she needs to find new customers," Drew speaks my exact thoughts. Drew is a graphic designer. He works for a small company that makes websites for companies. They made mine a few months ago.

I nod. "He's right. I do."

"My friend owns a marketing company. They mostly do clothing stuff, but I could ask them," Hutch offers.

I pat his back. "Thanks. That might help."

"Too bad it's so hard to get into that City Bake-Off competition. I heard they are televising it this year," Carly says as she makes an "x" on the tic-tac-toe board that Bray drew on a napkin. Ava claps and draws an "o."

"I won," she says with a big grin. "Can I go get the bubbles now?"

"Come on, squirt. Let's go grab them," Bray says as he sets her on the chair and turns. She gets on his back, piggyback-style, and they head downstairs.

The rooftop becomes quiet. Everyone seems to be trying to come up with an idea.

"You could try to see if you could get a sponsor for it. They pair smaller bakeries with big ones, right?" Gray asks. Roxy sits on his lap. They both look at me. Damn, I love these people. I feel so lucky to have them all on my team.

Al clears his throat and I look over at him. He looks...worried.

"What?" I ask.

"Cam," Al starts and pauses as if he isn't sure what to say and that's not like him at all.

"What's wrong?" I ask, setting my glass down as I step toward him.

"I have to tell you something," he says and I can hear the hesitation in his voice.

I wait, not saying a word, partly out of curiosity and partly out of respect for a man who I've come to love as much as my own grandfather.

"I know Edward McDowell Senior," he says, letting out a long breath and putting his hands up in a shrug.

It's as if his exhale prevents me from inhaling. I had to have heard that wrong. There's no way Al knows the son of the founder of the company that is trying to take down my café. Their website, which I may or may not have stalked, tells the history of John McDowell starting a bakery in the early nineteen hundreds. His son, Edward, took the company national and then global. Edward's son, Edward Jr., then continued the expansion and now is training his three sons to run it. Fletcher would be the youngest of the three.

"What?" I manage as my brain tries to reject what my ears have heard.

He gives another sheepish shrug and one corner of his mouth lifts a little. "Ed played poker with me years ago. I've known Fletch since he was a baby."

I blink because how is this possible. Then I groan because of course Al knows them. Fucking hell. Al knows everyone. He's like the mayor of the smallest town in one of the biggest cities.

"Al!" I groan, followed by a chorus of groans from everyone else.

He throws his hands up in the air. "Sorry. I...wasn't sure how to tell you." He pauses as I continue to wrap my head around Al knowing my rivals.

"I tried to talk some sense into him. I did. But Fletch is, well, he's very stubborn," Al concedes.

"No shit," I mutter under my breath.

"But I'm on Team Cam. We'll figure out a way. All of us will," he says as he motions to our apartment building with his head.

"Maybe I can find a sponsor for that bake-off?" I muse and then launch into what I could bake if I can find a partner bakery to pair with.

"Hold up," Gray says. "Explain this competition again."

"So, every year the city has this giant competition. It's being televised this year. The premise is that you get paired with a more established bakery that sponsors you, sort of like a mentor situation. Anyhow, the winner gets fifty thousand dollars to invest in their company and they get a free advertising plan from this big marketing firm and ten thousand to spend on some of the plan. It's a really big deal. Plus, you obviously get bragging rights. All the bakeries that have won have gone on to be huge. Bakeries from across the country come to compete. Last year's winner was this little food truck bakery and they were able to open two storefronts after their win," I explain.

"So, let's find you a sponsor," Al states. I cannot believe this man knows the McDowells, but also, I am totally not surprised.

If anyone here knows a company owner that could sponsor me, it'll be Al.

"Any company but McDowell's," I add.

Al's face falls. "I was going to suggest them. Are you sure? They would be a great match. They've opened bakeries and café storefronts all across the world. They are a huge company now," Al says.

I swallow. He's right. They are. And if Fletcher McDowell hadn't been the biggest jerk in the history of jerks, I'd consider that, but now, out of spite mostly and pride, I could never consider working with his family's company. Could I?

No. Absolutely not. Hard pass.

"I...I think that would be a bad idea," I say as I think of Fletcher. He epitomizes everything I hate, from his pretentious-looking suit to his perfectly sculpted hair that looks unkempt yet model-like all in one. Yeah, there's no way. Even if I entertained that, I don't see how we wouldn't kill each other. The look he gave me the other day tells me he loathes me just as much as I loathe him. It's a mutual-enemy situation.

"You know what they say," Hutch pipes up. Everyone turns to him. "Keep your friends close and your enemies closer."

CHAPTER SIX

Fletch

"I have no idea how to approach her?" I admit as I stare down the street toward Cam's Café. There has been a steady line of customers there all morning, even with the light snow falling. I turn back to our store and look around. Our general contractor finally got his crews working, and I'm seeing progress for the first time in weeks.

"You need to go talk to her. The show is going to decide contestants in a few weeks. I think you have to have all the paperwork in at the end of next week," Spencer says, his gaze following mine.

"I know," I growl, feeling in an even worse mood than I was when we arrived this morning.

"So, who are we going to get to run the kitchen here?" he asks as he looks around us.

I sigh. "I need to go through our applicants again. Dalton had a recommendation of a chef who was his second choice for the last property."

"I think that dude had some issues though," Spencer points out.

I grimace. Damn. What a mess! "I'm going for a walk," I declare. "I need to clear my head."

"Good luck," Spencer calls out after me with a chuckle.

I flick him off and start down the street toward the park. The snowfall is actually sort of nice. It's painting the city in a light layer of white that looks picturesque. I get to the metal wrought-iron trellis at the entry of the park. A bench sits just off to the side a few paces into the trail. Even with the snow, it's a lovely, serene place.

Then I hear a noise, a sort of rustling, followed by a grunt. I search the forested area and see a man in full camo emerge from...a duck blind. Wait? Are duck blinds even legal in the city?

He pulls off his face covering and I blink. I swear this man looks just like Hutchinson Cromwell, the former linebacker of our football team.

"Hey," he says as he strides past me, peeling back several layers to show off some tattoos and a very trendy-looking shirt. He somehow pulls off a manbun situation as if it's the coolest thing in the world.

"Uh, hey," I manage.

He's an enormous brute of a human, towering over me by nearly a half foot, which is saying something because I'm not a short person. He looks like a Viking mixed with a duck hunter mixed with a bartender.

"You're that McDowell guy," he says and it's not a question. Damn, I guess my reputation precedes me.

"Guilty," I reply.

He steps forward and now he's in my space. Fuck. I hope this isn't Cam's bodyguard, because this guy could crush me in a single hand.

He points to my chest. "Don't fuck with Cam. Also, you

should sponsor her café for that bake-off thing. It's the least you can do since you are trying to steal her customers," he says.

I'm shocked into silence. Wait? Did he just suggest the same idea I was contemplating?

I swallow. "I was actually going to ask her about that, but, uh, well, we aren't exactly on great terms. And..." I trail off. I'm still considering if I can even work with this woman without wanting to strangle her, or worse, she might strangle me.

He starts laughing and holds out his hand. "I'm Hutch Cromwell, by the way," he says as we shake hands.

"I sort of figured that one out," I huff.

He chuckles again and steps back, nodding toward Cam's Café. "Cam is a fireball. She just might be the most stubborn human I know, but she also has the biggest heart. When I had the flu last year, she made me homemade chicken dumpling soup and biscuits. She also dropped a care package of medicine off at my door every day for a full week. So if you hurt her in any way, I will kill you and bury you out here where no one will find you." I grimace. "But her café is amazing. She's the best baker I've ever met. Her café deserves the recognition. Maybe, just maybe, there's a way your two companies can coexist. I'm not the man to figure out those logistics, but perhaps you're smarter than me when it comes to that sort of thing."

"Any other words of wisdom?" I inquire.

"Nope. But good luck," he says with another laugh. He motions to the café with his head. "You're going to need it."

He starts to walk away and then turns back to me doing that two-fingers-to-his-eyes-and-then-mine motion. "Don't forget, I will level anyone who hurts my friends."

"Yeah, got that," I mumble.

He gives me a friendly wave and smiles as if he didn't just

threaten me with bodily harm. And what the hell was he doing in the park?

God, this is a weird-ass place. I decide today isn't the day to provoke Cam Tanner. I start back toward the street and see Al crossing from Cam's Café to his apartment building.

He also waves at Hutchinson Cromwell who is entering the café. Does everyone here know each other?

"Fletch, how are you?" Al says warmly as he approaches me.

"Oh, I'm OK, I suppose," I reply because honestly, I'm not sure how I feel about what just transpired. It's not every day a former linebacker threatens your life and also gives you advice all in the same conversation.

Al frowns as he opens the apartment building door. "Come on up. Let's chat."

It's either chat with Al or go back to the office and stare at the ceiling while no good ideas pop in my head, so I guess Al's offer is the more appealing of the two.

"Just for a few minutes," I state, not sure how long I want to stay. I almost text Spencer to call me in fifteen minutes and pretend there's an office crisis, but for reasons I can't explain, I don't.

I follow Al to the elevator. "Uh, does that thing work?" I ask.

He smirks. "Didn't work a few weeks ago, but it's all fixed now. Don't be chicken. Come on," he teases.

Now he's just tapped into my competitive nature, one sculpted by being the youngest of three brothers and five male cousins. I get inside and we ride up to the top floor.

It opens into a private foyer and Al unlocks one side of a set of double doors and ushers me inside.

"How about a drink?" Al suggests, shuffling over to one of those giant globes that's actually a liquor cabinet. He pulls out a bottle of whiskey, and damn if it isn't a really good bottle from a small distillery in Scotland. The man does have a penchant for poker and really good alcohol.

He holds up the bottle and I nod as he pours us both a glass. I look around his apartment. I haven't been here in years. Everything is still straight out of an antique store, which makes sense since his late wife owned one. I miss Edith's cooking. She always had something cooking, stewing, or baking when I'd visit as a kid with my grandfather. I partly wonder if I open that cupboard by the television there would still be coloring books and games in there. I suspect there would be as nothing else has changed in here in the last thirty years.

"You need to sponsor Cam's Café in the City Bake-Off," he states as he sits and crosses a leg.

What the hell is it with everyone? Is there a conspiracy I'm not aware of?

"So I hear," I reply as I sit down on a chair near him.

"Oh?" he asks, raising one big, bushy eyebrow.

"I just had the...pleasure of meeting Hutchinson Cromwell," I explain.

Al starts laughing. "Oh, Hutch. Hope he didn't threaten to pummel you too much."

I give him a deadpan look and he keeps laughing. "Laugh it up. That man could crush me with one hand."

Al waves me off. "Hutch wouldn't hurt a fly. I'm surprised he even played football. Anyhow, he's right. You should."

"Cam and I sort of...I'm not sure it's the right thing to do." I stumble over my words, not wanting to admit the ill-tempered beauty across the street has somehow penetrated my armor.

Shrugging, Al takes another drink. "Let me work on her. But no funny business, Fletch. This is a serious agreement. Cam's Café is a beacon of light in this neighborhood. I'm all for some friendly competition, but I think you need to differentiate your store from hers. Remember that store you guys did in...oh, where was it? Oh, Paris."

I nod. The Paris location was a really tough one. We had to brand ourselves as the location for cupcakes and matcha because the neighborhood already was filled with patisseries and cafés that served coffee way better than we could possibly dream of providing.

"So what could we provide?" I contemplate aloud.

"Maybe, if you sponsor Cam, you'll learn where she excels so you can figure that out?" he suggests. "You could coexist in harmony. Stranger things have happened."

"If you say so," I mumble as I finish my drink and consider if harmony with Cam could exist in this world. Somehow, I'm highly doubting that, but also, deep down, I'd love to get to know this intriguing woman. If our worlds hadn't collided in the way they had, maybe, in another universe, we'd get along. Maybe.

CHAPTER SEVEN

Cam

I pull my latest batch of cookies from the oven and set them on the rack to cool. It's my third attempt in as many days to try to make this cookie recipe that Drew and I dreamed up over margaritas five nights ago.

"It puts the rum in the coconut!" Drew shouts as he dances around our kitchen table. What started out as a search for my missing salt-shaker has turned into a night of drinking.

I fall down laughing. "OK, Hannibal Lecter of the witch coven."

"Oh my God! Don't be such a beotch!" he says, drawing out the last word. I throw a lime at him and it hits him in the head.

"Hey! Don't hurt my money maker!" he cries out, rubbing his forehead.

Now, I'm full-on rolling around on the floor. "Your." Laugh. "Money." Laugh. "Maker." Laugh.

"What? How will I find my sugar daddy if you bruise this perfection?" he says, sighing as he dramatically waves a hand in front of his face.

"You are the sugar daddy!" I laugh.

He giggles and hiccups, raising his glass in the air and letting the margarita spill on the floor. "To sugar daddies!"

"To tequila!" I say as I sit up and we clink glasses.

"You need a margarita cookie," he declares after taking a sip of his strawberry margarita.

I purse my lips. "That's actually a good idea." I pull my phone from my pocket and make a note so I don't forget it tomorrow.

"What are you doing? Sexting?" Drew asks.

I glare up at him. "Who am I going to sext?"

"Max." He waggles his eyebrows.

I roll my eyes. "No way. He's been friend-zoned. I'm making a note about the cookie idea. It's not a bad idea."

"You can call it, the Strawberry Drewgarita," he says, motioning with his hands as if the words will magically appear in the air in front of him.

I groan and throw another lime at him. But I also smile. Drew always makes me smile. Thank God for good friends.

A strawberry margarita cookie with lime frosting. It sounded simple and delicious. But I can't perfect the strawberry cookie no matter how hard I try.

I desperately want to try them right now, because I feel like this batch might be the one, but they need to cool. So, I walk to the front of my café. Adriana is helping customers and I decide to go and change out the menu. Another week, another list of cookie and coffee specials.

I head into my tiny office and print a new specials menu while trying not to think about Fletcher McDowell. I need to start growing my profit if I'm going to make my goals for the year. And right now, McDowell's moving in down the street may hamper my ability to grow this business that I've spent years working to own. And worse, it could completely decimate us. The next closest bakery, café, or coffeehouse is at least four blocks away.

I step back into the café, a handful of copies of the menu in my hand, one for the outside and a few for the bar area. I'm looking down to double-check my spelling when all of a sudden I run smack into a body.

The papers go flying and strong hands clutch my upper arms, keeping me from face-planting. My hand goes to chiseled pectoral muscles as I steady myself.

"Whoa," a deep voice says, a deep voice that I immediately recognize.

I look up, and for reasons I cannot explain, anger begins to boil inside me like a witch's cauldron. I shove off him and step back. I hate that I just pushed against a perfect set of abdominals. I hate that he looks like a model in a perfume commercial without even trying. And I hate the smug look on his face.

"I have a proposition for you," he starts. I open my mouth to speak but he puts up a hand. "Not that one. A new one."

My mouth opens and closes a few times because now I'm confused. It's like this statement just caused my brain to short-circuit. What the hell does he mean, a new one? God, does this man ever stop?

"Not interested," I reply through gritted teeth.

"Oh, come on. Hear me out. I swear, I come in peace," he says while flashing me some kind of smile that I am pretty sure is reserved for charming women, but he has no idea that I am above all such man maneuvers.

"Get out!" I say loudly, not even caring if other customers hear.

"Cam, please listen," he says trying again.

"God! You really have some audacity, don't you? You think you're so special, so high and mighty. Well, I'll let you in on a little secret. You aren't impressive. You aren't going to *win me over* with some desperate ploy to *help me*. I'm doing just fine." OK, that's a blatant lie, but he doesn't need to know that. "In fact, I'm doing better than fine. Your store isn't going to be able to keep up with mine. So best of luck. Now, get the fuck out of my store and don't come back. I'm banning you from entering this property. The next time I see you in here, I'll be calling the police. Now leave," I growl as I point to the door.

He looks at me and sets a piece of paper down on the bar. "Please consider a sponsorship from us for the upcoming competition," he offers. "My number is on the back." And without any further explanation, he turns and walks out of my café.

"What was that about?" Adriana asks.

Sighing, I grab the paper and toss it in the trash can behind the counter.

"Nothing. McDowell's thinks that they can buy us out, but they have another thing coming. I'm not going down without a fight," I explain.

"Oh, right, but what did he mean about a sponsorship?" she asks.

I lean on the counter, placing my hands on the cool marble in hopes that calms me down. "Ever heard of the City Bake-Off?" I ask.

"Yeah. It's huge. They are even televising it. Why?" she asks.

"You have to get a sponsorship to enter. But I'm definitely not going to accept one from McDowell's," I state dryly.

"Why not?" she asks.

"Adriana, seriously? They are the competition! I bet that agreement would have a bunch of caveats that end my store. It'd be just like Fletcher to do that," I say as if I know the man personally. But hell, I know him enough to know I can't trust him, or at least I shouldn't.

"But if you can win the competition, then we could get enough new customers to fend off a takeover or a major loss in profit," she points out, and I hate that she isn't wrong. I want that all to be wrong. I want to be the David to McDow-ell's Goliath. I want to be the underdog that wins.

My phone buzzes and I look down to see a text from Winston, my older brother. He texts once a week. Always on a Thursday. If anything, Winston is a man of routine.

Winston: So, what's your marketing game plan? Any ideas yet?

He knows about McDowell's. He's offered a hundred different ideas, but none that would work. I hate that my family views this debacle as another failure of mine, that they all have to swoop in and save the day. I want so badly to prove that I can do this. I'm tired of all of them babying me.

I lean down and pick up the document from the trash. Without another word to Adriana, I walk back into the office, stopping to grab a margarita cookie off the cooling rack, and I shut the door. I take a bite of the cookie once I'm seated.

Holy shitballs! This one came out perfect. I smirk. McDowell's doesn't have a margarita cookie. But Cam's Café does. I look down at the paper on my desk. A part of me still wants to toss it in the trash, but I'd be lying if I said I wasn't curious. What's he playing at?

I guess there's only one way to find out. I lean forward and begin to read.

Let's see what Fletcher McDowell is offering. It's prob-ably a contract with the devil himself, but maybe, just maybe, I can use it to turn the tables. Can I outwit my rival? Possibly. Although I'm talking about a multinational corporation with a team of lawyers, so the odds aren't in my favor. But I have one thing that Fletcher doesn't have...an entire building of supporters right across the street.

CHAPTER EIGHT

Fletch

I stare out at the city. Our company's headquarters are located on the top five floors of this twenty-eight-story building.

I watch the little ant-like people walking on the streets below. In the distance, I can just barely make out Hearts Lane Park. I wonder what Cam Tanner is up to today. Did she read my contract? Is she considering it?

I smirk at the memory of her telling me I was permanently banned from her store. She acts all feisty with her fighting words, but somehow based on my conversations with Al and that Hutch guy, I think she's actually a giant softy. I just don't know how to break that outer hard candy shell to get to the gooey center.

I turn back around and take in my office with its expensive furniture and high-tech communications. I've never known any different. My grandfather took the company public before I was born. He expanded it globally and managed to stay at the helm of the board. He was so successful that the board easily voted in my father when the time came. I suppose they thought the apple didn't fall far from the tree.

And I'm sure they'd vote for Spencer or Dalton, but definitely not me. I ruined my chances of that years ago. No amount of success can undo an internet search.

I curse my younger self under my breath as I walk back to my desk and sit down. God, I was an idiot. I'd blame it on youth, but I knew I was fucking up even back then. I just didn't care. I was so self-centered.

People expect me to be that way still. But somehow, when our mom had a cancer scare and Dad called to tell me, I just changed. In an instant, I realized none of the people around me were my real friends or family. I got on a plane from Ibiza and went straight to see her.

Realizing I could lose a family member snapped me out of it, whatever *it* was. Fortunately, Mom was fine. At Mom's encouragement, Dad offered me a shit job at the company and I took it. For the first time, I wanted to be a McDowell. Not just for the perks, but because I wanted to be part of something bigger than me.

I study the plans for the new store that are lying on my desk. I'm supposed to approve them, but my mind keeps drifting back to Camryn. The contract I had our lawyers draw up wasn't as harsh as I originally had wanted.

It provides for the sponsorship. We get to keep any recipes developed for the show for exclusive use at our stores, which will of course be attributed to her. If she wins, she gets to keep all the money. If she loses, we get a fifty-fifty stake in her company with the ability for her to buy us out after five years. Now, it will only take one year to put her out of business, but who's counting?

Dad wanted us to take full ownership, but I know she wouldn't even consider that.

I'm about to head over to the store to see our progress when I see a text.

Unknown: I have my own terms and conditions. I can meet you at your store at three today.

One hundred percent Camryn. But I also want to fuck with her.

Me: Who is this?

Unknown: Seriously? (glaring emoji)

Me: Seriously.

Unknown: Three P.M. Fucker.

I laugh out loud.

Me: I'll make sure to be prompt, Ms. Tanner.

Unknown: Try bringing some manners as well.

Me: I'll have you know, I am the epitome of manners.

Unknown: (laughing-out-loud emoji)

Unknown: Wait. Were you serious?

Me: I'm always serious.

Unknown: Interesting. Not what Page 6 had to say about you when I looked you up.

Me: Looking me up? Interesting.

Unknown: (angry face) Don't flatter yourself. I always research who I may OR MAY NOT be doing business with. Or do you not know what research is?

Me: Not personally. I have people who do that for me.

Unknown: Shocking.

Me: See you at three.

Unknown: Yeah. See you.

I put the phone down and smile. I'm going to have so much fun fucking with Ms. Tanner. I wonder how many buttons of hers I can press? It's almost like a challenge, a quest. If only I could find someone to date who could provide me with such witty banter. On the other hand, I'd probably want to kill them. Bring it on, Camryn. At least I know you'd never date a man like me and quid pro quo.

———

I have the foreman give me a final tour of the kitchen area, which is coming together after a month's delay. I've chosen the opening day for three months from now. It'll allow us to get through this competition and then know the game plan for how we are going to proceed here on Hearts Lane.

A woman clears her throat from behind me and I turn to see Camryn. I look at my watch. It's five till three.

"You're early," I state.

"Early is on time. On time is late," she says as her eyes bore into me.

"Touché," I retort. I motion to some stools over by a table where building plans are rolled up and stacked to one side.

Camryn unfurls a document and sets it on the table. "My counteroffer," she says as she pushes it toward me.

"I don't believe I said I would entertain a counteroffer, Ms. Tanner," I say as I push the paper back toward her.

Her cheeks turn dark pink. I smirk. I have already flustered her. I'll take the point.

"Well, I never said I was agreeing to your terms, Mr. McDowell. So, *this* is my counteroffer," she says as she taps on the paper.

Curiosity gets the best of me and I snatch the document from her and read through it. She's kept most things the same except she's made it a fifty-one percent ownership that she retains in her store and we pay off her loan. Interesting. I look at the loan amount. It's six figures, but peanuts for us.

"That's a big loan," I say with a raised eyebrow, deciding to play coy.

She rolls her eyes. "Last year, McDowell's made five

hundred million dollars in profit. You are projected to exceed that by nearly one hundred million this year. You own approximately four hundred stores with another twenty scheduled to open this year. I hardly think that sum of money would make anyone blink." She motions around us. "Hell, you probably spent that in here during the first two weeks of renovations."

She's not far off. For reasons I can't explain, I say, "Fine. Accepted. But I'm adding a clause that you need to get someone to run your store during the competition. I want your full focus on our team winning. We've never lost when we sponsor someone."

She swallows and I wonder if my new stipulation will cause an issue.

"Fine," she says after a beat.

I hold out my hand and she slowly raises hers to mine. I close my fingers around hers and we shake. I can't help enjoying the feeling of her smaller hand in mine. Her skin is incredibly soft and smooth. I wonder for the briefest of moments if her skin is that smooth everywhere.

"I'll have my team draw up the official contract and courier it over to you," I state as I stand.

"Wonderful," she says.

"And we start working on recipes in two days," I add as she begins walking toward the door. Her step falters and I know she's surprised by the word *we*.

She turns and looks up at me. "*We?*"

"Yes. *We*. As in, you and me," I restate as I fight not to smirk.

"I-I didn't realize you'd be so...involved," she adds.

I shrug. "I like to see my investments in action. You understand, right?"

She glares at me and I know she already regrets agreeing to this, but I also know she needs to do this competition and no other company is knocking down her door. I saw to that with a few simple calls.

"Fine. Saturday night. After I close," she says.

"I'll see you at nine," I say and I see the look of irritation because she hates that I know she closes at nine on Thursdays.

She doesn't say another word as she turns and walks out of the building. I watch her walk down the street where she stops to talk to a woman and a little girl. They all seem to know each other as Cam picks up the little girl and hugs her. Then they all walk over to her store. I wonder who they are for the briefest of moments. But then I remember that I just won. This is going to help me figure her out, and by keeping my enemy close, I'll find the chink in her armor. You're about to go down, Ms. Tanner.

CHAPTER NINE

Cam

I sip my martini and snuggle up in one of the blankets that Al keeps up here for the winter happy hours. He has all the heaters going and the fire pit.

I glance down at my phone to see if Max has messaged me back. He's been busy lately and I hate admitting I miss our little text chats, but I do. I grin when I see he's replied.

Max: Sorry. Crazy schedule today. So, how's your business situation going?

Me: I'm going to do a project with that business.

Max: You are?

Me: Yeah. There's this thing that came up and we're going to work as a team.

Max: Do you think that's a good idea?

Me: (shrugging emoji)

Max: You didn't sign anything yet, did you?

Me: (sheepish emoji)

Max: E! Why would you do that?

I grin. I love when he calls me "E."

Me: The only way forward is through.

Max: I hope you have a plan.

Me: Sort of.

Max: We should talk later. I have to go to some event. Don't sign any other contracts tonight, OK?

I laugh.

Me: I'll try not to.

I look around at my friends and neighbors.

Jessa and Troy are deep in conversation with Margie and Cornelia, and Drew is perched on the arm of one of the oversized deck chairs that Margie is sitting in. They are having some debate about whether an actor from a show they all used to watch is still alive or not.

"He's dead," Drew announces as he holds up his phone. They all sigh and immediately launch into a morbid eulogy of sorts with each of them naming their favorite show or film the actor was in.

I glance at the bar. Roxy is sitting in Gray's lap as they both watch some funny video on her social media while Al makes her another drink. Piper is in Kasen's lap. She's sketching something in a notebook while Kasen chats with Hutch. Roxy's employee, Jocelyn, is up here tonight. She's standing by Hutch explaining why a character in her favorite book is better than the one in his favorite book.

Bray is sitting on the end seat with Ava in his lap. He's half participating in their favorite bar game of tic-tac-toe while he chats with Carly. I swear those two have the hots for each other. I mean they already practically raise Ava as a couple without being a couple. Weird.

Everything seems so normal. Yet, I feel…distant. Like I'm watching all of this in a film instead of being a part of it.

"What's eating you, kid?" Al asks as he leans over the bar to pour more martini into my glass. He drops two olives in there for good measure and stands back as he assesses me.

"I signed the contract," I announce.

The space falls silent.

"Wait. What?" Drew asks. "When were you going to tell us this?" I cringe a little. I had wanted to call him but he's been so supportive of my fight against McDowell's that I knew he'd talk me out of it and I really need this. Fletch had made one change from our agreed-upon stipulations, a lien on my equipment for two years. If the café goes belly up, he would be able to retain them for sale to pay off the money spent on covering my loan. I admit I don't love being tied to the McDowell's any more than I already am, but it seemed fair and Winston didn't have any major issues with that when we chatted.

I sigh as I take in everyone's faces. Are they disappointed in me? "I just did it. Before coming up here. He had it couriered over this afternoon."

"And you didn't think to mention this to anyone here?" Margie asks. "Did you have a lawyer look it over?"

"Yes. Winston looked at it," I say. My big brother is a lawyer for a nonprofit that rescues animals.

"Are dogs involved?" Drew asks, his voice laced with sarcasm.

I glare at him.

"I thought you'd all be happy. I'm going to be in the City Bake-Off competition. I'll be on television. This is huge for Cam's Café," I explain.

"We thought you were going to bring McDowell's down, not join with them," Hutch states to a round of nods from my friends.

"Keep your enemies closer, right?" I say with a shrug.

"I hope you know what you're doing," Bray says with a look of concern. Shit. Now, I'm worried. Did I just make a deal with the devil himself? Possibly. But can I flip the script on him? Also possible.

"Listen. The new plan is to get close to Fletcher McDowell and then find his weak spot and exploit the hell out of it," I explain.

"Like counterintelligence?" Kasen asks.

"Exactly. If I can learn more about what they plan to sell at this new place down the street, then I can change up things at the café in a way that hurts their bottom dollar. Plus, I got them to pay off my small business loan," I say with a grin.

"No way," Hutch says.

"Way," I reply and he gives me a high five.

"OK, that's one thing," he says.

"Exactly. Now, I need to come up with a cookie, a cupcake, and a pie for this competition," I say as I grab some chips from a bowl on the bar.

"Chocolate," Ava says without looking up from where she's making the tenth tic-tac-toe board on a napkin.

"Cookies?" I ask.

"All of them," she says.

"S'mores," Carly suggests.

"Oh, yeah. Mom's right, s'mores," Ava says, looking up this time to give me a big grin.

"I'll consider that one. Any other brilliant idea?" I ask as I look around.

"Something with alcohol," Cornelia says as she raises a glass of wine.

"Yeah, something with bourbon or whiskey," Troy chimes in. And just like that, everyone is saying flavors from bubblegum to lingonberry. I type notes on my phone, hoping that one of these crazy flavors will lead to a brilliant idea because those strawberry margarita cookies were a hit.

By the time happy hour dies down, I'm feeling better and more confident in my decision.

"You know, Fletcher isn't a horrible human," Al says as he wipes the bar clean.

I laugh, which comes out more like a snort. "Right."

He gives me a pointed look. "He's not, Camryn. He's a good kid. He lost his way for a bit, but he's made up for lost time. He's a decent young man. I think you both have a lot in common."

This time I laugh harder. "Al, we have nothing in common aside from running competing businesses."

He shakes his head. "You are both youngest siblings looking to prove yourselves. You are both stubborn. You both love your family. And you're both very driven when you want something. But you also are both fiercely loyal and kind to those you love."

I find all of those things very hard to believe, but I know Al won't back down, so I just nod. "OK, Al."

He walks around the bar and pats my knee. "I'm serious, Cam. Give the guy a chance. I think if you combined your talents, you'd be a force to be reckoned with. No one would be able to beat you at this competition."

"I plan on winning it," I state. With or without Fletcher McDowell.

"Good. I look forward to watching you do just that," he says with a warm smile. "You're a talented baker. I know you can win this."

I hop off my stool and hug him. He pats my back. "Now, go figure out the winning recipes. I'm always here to try them out."

I giggle and pull away. "And here I thought Ava would be my only taste tester."

"The kid can't have all the fun," he says as we walk to the

door. He turns while we're on the stairs. "Just remember what I said. Fletch isn't a bad guy."

"OK," I manage but inside I'm seriously doubting this. And why is Al pushing it? Fletcher probably puts on some show for family and friends. He seems like the type of person to manipulate people in that way.

I walk down to my apartment and find Drew sitting on the sofa, clearly just out of the shower. The man showers in two minutes flat, which is shocking considering how long he takes to do his hair. He literally just left the rooftop five minutes ago.

"So, what the hell, Cam?" he says, and I know I'm in trouble.

I sit across from him in my cozy chair and curl my legs beneath me. "I'm sorry. I told you I was considering his offer. I just didn't see it till this afternoon and I sent it to Winston and then I...signed it." He gives me a knowing look. "Fine. I knew you'd try to talk me out of it and I wanted to make this decision all on my own."

"But why? You know I'm always here for you," he says and I hate he sounds hurt.

"Because one, if something goes wrong, I don't want to feel like it's your fault for talking me into or out of something. And two, for once, I wanted to make a business decision all on my own. I love your advice. I cherish it, but this was something that I needed to do alone," I try to explain.

I get up and walk over to him, plopping down on the sofa and leaning my head on his shoulder. "Please don't be mad. I really need to take ownership of this all alone. It's important to me that I did this. I made this decision," I try again to put my thoughts into words.

"Promise me something," he says.

I pause and wait for his request.

"If Fletcher so much as walks an inch out of line, you tell

me. I will pummel his uppity ass, OK?" he says and I shake with laughter.

"Fine. That I can agree to," I say as I hold out my hand and we do our secret handshake, the one we came up with while drinking together one night many years ago.

"Love ya, Drew. Thank you for always wanting the best for me," I say because I do. This man has stuck with me through so many things. He's my rock.

"Love you, too, you crazy beotch." He pauses and I wonder if he's going to keep laying into me, but instead, he says, "Now, let's figure out these competition-winning flavors. We have a major corporation to take down."

"Yes, let's do that," I agree as we begin going through the notes I took upstairs, looking for inspiration. But as we discuss flavors, I keep thinking about what Al said. There's no way Fletcher can be a good guy. He's the villain in my story, right? A crazy, good-looking villain. A villain that I might sleep with if I lost my good judgment. But a villain nonetheless.

CHAPTER TEN

Fletch

I knock on the door to Cam's Café for a second time. Cam had confirmed that I should meet her here at nine fifteen sharp. It's now nine seventeen.

The door to the back of the café opens and Cam appears. She's backlit by the light in the kitchen. Her red hair looks ethereal.

She slowly walks to the door and for a long moment we stare at each other through the glass. Finally, she unlocks the door and pushes it open.

I step inside and smell something wonderful. Raising my face into the air, I sniff. "What is that?"

She grins. "I'd tell you, but then I'd have to kill you."

"Sounds ominous," I retort.

She shrugs and I follow her into the kitchen.

She places her hands on her hips and motions to three plates.

"Cranberry cupcakes with orange frosting." She points to

some cupcakes. "Everything-but-the-kitchen-sink pepper-mint cookies." She motions to a plate of cookies and a pie. "A pine soda pie."

I raise an eyebrow. "Pine soda?"

She nods. "I heard the theme is childhood Christmas memories. My mom always made orange cinnamon rolls and I used to like to eat them with some candied cranberries. Peppermint candy canes were my fave. And my grandmother always made a pine soda pie. I don't have her recipe, so this is my twist on it."

Interesting. The fact that she shared these things with me feels very...intimate as if we're on a date. For the briefest of moments, I wonder what her family is like. Does her family have one of those big American holiday parties that you see in movies? Did her grandmother live with her family? A dozen questions pop into my head but I don't ask a single one. Instead, I step forward.

She motions for me to try one. I take a bite of a cupcake because the orange smell is calling to me. I hold back a groan. Damn. This is good.

I chew and am surprised by little pops in my mouth. I swallow. "Is that...are the cranberries..." I trail off as I examine the cupcake more closely.

"I candied the cranberries first and then dipped them in powdered sugar so they wouldn't sink to the bottom," she explains. I've heard of pastry chefs rolling things like blue-berries in flour to prevent them from sinking, but this is genius.

I nod and set the cupcake down. I move on to the cookie. I take a bite. Shockingly, the peppermint isn't as overpow-ering as I thought it would be. There's just a hint of it.

I look over at her. "I did the smallest amount of crushed peppermint. I didn't think people would want to be overpow-ered." She pauses and reaches over, taking a bite of one of them. She chews it and tilts her head to one side as if contemplating something.

"What?" I ask.

"I'm not a hundred percent about this one. I like it, but peppermint is a strong flavor. I might lose some judges with it. What do you think?" she asks.

I nod. She's not wrong. "I agree. Maybe we consider a different cookie just to be safe."

She reaches over and cuts a piece of pie and sets it on a plate with a fork. She pushes it over to me after adding a dollop of what looks to be homemade whipped cream.

I examine it, still unsure about this one. With a slight shrug, I take a bite. It's shockingly good, like really good.

"This is great," I admit begrudgingly.

She smiles, and with another fork, she takes a small bite right from the pie. She grins. "Gan-gan would be proud."

"Gan-gan?" I ask, fighting a smirk.

She blushes and the color of pink roses coats her ivory skin. I watch it bloom across her neck and I wonder if it goes all the way to her breasts which are covered by the T-shirt she's wearing. I give my head a little shake to clear my thoughts. I absolutely cannot think about her that way. What the hell is wrong with me?

"That's what we called my grandmother." Her blush grows a little darker. "I couldn't say Grandma."

I smirk. "You seem to have recently mastered it. Well done, you."

The blush dissipates and she glares at me.

"So, what are we going to do for the cookie?" I ask, deciding to ignore her cute angry stare.

She whips around and pulls a tray of cookies off her cooling rack. She places it in front of me.

"What am I looking at here?"

"I read an article about your family and it inspired this cookie," she states as she motions to the cookies.

I give her a curious look. "What article?"

She pulls a phone out of the pocket of her apron and passes it to me. I scan an article from about ten years ago. I don't remember this at all, but then again, I was probably tripping balls on a Caribbean island or fucking two girls at once on the family yacht. I grimace at the memories. The article was mostly interviewing my mother about holiday traditions in the McDowell family. She mentioned eggnog.

"Eggnog?" I ask, memories are falling from the far corners of my mind. It was something we always had at the holidays. We didn't have many traditions but that was most definitely one of them.

She nods. I bite into a cookie. It definitely has an eggnog taste to it and it also has a cinnamon-flavored frosting with little gold flecks. And fuck, this is a good cookie.

"This is the one," I state as I finish the cookie and grab another. "How did you get the cookie to mimic the eggnog flavor so well?"

She smirks. "I guess you'll have to wait and find out."

Now, it's me glaring at her. "You know by contract I get the recipes, right?"

She nods. "Yep."

I feel my jaw clenching. This woman drives me insane.

"Fine," I say sighing. "I'll approve these three recipes. But we should come up with a fourth one in case of a bake-off tiebreaker round."

She nods. "What else do you remember from the holidays?"

"I don't know. I'm not a holiday type of person," I admit. I start thinking and truly I don't remember a lot about holidays. My parents always threw a big holiday party for friends and family. We often went to our beach house in the

Caribbean for New Year's. There were always lavish gifts. But not a ton of traditions.

Then a single memory comes to the front of the pack. "Gingerbread," I state as I look over at her.

Her lips twitch and I can tell she's fighting a grin, but the smile wins and spreads across her face. I realize I haven't seen her smile before, not really. She's breathtaking like this. She should always be smiling.

"I love it. We used to make gingerbread houses at my gan-gan's house," she says, her smile widening.

"We used to make them too. Well, my brothers mostly made them and I just sat and ate the candy and gingerbread men," I admit.

She giggles and now I'm fighting a smile. "Same. My brother is a lot older than me. I think he would get frustrated with my childish antics. I loved eating those little cinnamon candies and the gumdrops."

"Red or green?" I ask, raising an eyebrow in a challenge.

"Red, of course."

I laugh. "So there is something we have in common."

She rolls her eyes. "What? I doubt it, aside from we are both humans, living in the same city, working in the same industry, we're both youngest siblings, we're both business people, both love eggnog and red gumdrops, and we both have a penchant for speaking before we think?"

Well, talk about feeling called out. "Fine, I guess we have about eight things in common."

"Oh my God, did we just become friends?" she asks sarcastically.

"Nope. No worries there, you are still my competitor except when we are working on this competition," I say, my jaw ticcing as I let her get to me again. I need to play it cool. I cannot let this woman win even one small battle.

"Fine, a truce only during our working hours together," she says as she holds out her hand.

I shake it. "Works for me. Speaking of working hours. I'm done for the night. I need you to send me a list of supplies. I'll have our staff stock them for the competition," I state as I head to the door.

"Anything else, sire?" she asks as she follows me.

"Sire? Really? That's the best you can do?"

She shrugs. "It's late. I'm sure I can be more irritating at our next meeting."

"Please see that you are," I say as I open the door. She walks up to me with a bag in her hand and I look at it.

"I boxed some of the things up in case you want any other taste testers," she explains.

I take the bag. "I think I should taste-test them all again. Just to be sure, of course."

She laughs. "Well, let me know any further thoughts, then."

"I will," I say as I leave, fighting the urge to smile. Why does this infuriating woman have to be so charming and witty? Part of that makes me hate her more, but I also feel a pull toward her in a way that I will not be letting myself explore.

I contemplate what just happened the entire drive home. Is Camryn Tanner not as bad as I thought? No. There's no way. Right?

CHAPTER ELEVEN

Cam

I pick up my wineglass and lean back into the oversized chair in Margie and Cornelia's apartment. "I can't do this," I state as I drown my sorrows in wine. It's only been twenty-four hours since I made the cookies for Fletcher McDowell and I'm already in deep regret about my decision to work with him.

"Sure you can," Margie encourages. "You're in the thick of it now. You just need to see it through, win the damn contest, and take all that money to invest in your business."

"No, you need to weasel your way onto his good side. Find out all the branding and menu stuff for that new store and then we rebrand you in a way that usurps anything they can do," Jocelyn says.

We all turn to look at her.

"What? I love a good rivals-to-lovers story," she says with a shrug.

"This isn't a rivals-to-lovers story, Joc. It's my actual life," I groan.

Cornelia pats my leg. "Sweets, you just need to focus on winning. Let us brainstorm ways to build your business. Margie and I have hoards of time on our hands, don't we?" She turns to her best friend.

"Speak for yourself. I have a date on Friday," Margie huffs as she reaches for her wineglass.

Roxy and Carly giggle and I roll my eyes. "Let's just talk about something else, anything else. I need to take my mind off the café for one night. I'm already nervous about leaving Adriana over there by herself tonight to close."

"She'll be fine. I mean I let Joc close all the time," Roxy teases and Jocelyn flicks her off.

"Hutch figure out who leaves those flowers every day on the park bench yet?" I ask.

Roxy shakes her head. "Nope. He thought it was Troy the other day. He followed him on his walk. And then Al and then Bray on one of his runs. Oh, and that guy who lives two doors down."

We all look at her with scrunched faces as we try to figure out which guy. "Who?" I ask.

"You know, that weird guy who always wears sweater vests even when it's summer," she says.

"Oh, that's Wayne. And yes, he is weird," Margie states.

"What about Herb or that woman..." Carly trails off as she thinks. "The one with the bright purple hair."

"Denise?" Margie asks.

"No. The other one," Carly says as there's a knock at the door. She gets up and opens it to let Jessa in.

"What'd I miss?" Jessa asks as Margie pours her some wine.

"We're guessing the flower person again," I state.

"Oh. I love that game. What about Mr. Jenkins next door?" Jessa asks.

"No, he's too grumpy," Jocelyn says. "I saw him push Licorice out of the way with his cane last week."

"What? If he so much as touches a hair on my baby's head again, I will throw down," Roxy says, her jaw clenching.

I start laughing. "Mr. Jenkins is like ninety. What are you going to do? Take his cane?"

She rolls her eyes. "No. But I'm not above yelling at him. I don't care if he's one hundred."

We're all quiet for a moment as we consider who it could be. Hutch has been so obsessed with this over the past year. I feel like he's using it as a distraction but I don't think anything is wrong in his life.

"Why does Hutch care so much about this?" I ask, voicing my thoughts aloud.

Everyone shrugs. "I think he's bored," Jocelyn says.

"Bored? He's always so busy. I think he wants to be the one that finds the answer," Roxy suggests.

"I think Hutch is a closet true crime fan," Carly muses.

"You all are crazy. Hutchinson is just a good boy trying to do a good deed," Margie declares.

We all giggle.

"I'm not sure he's all good. Didn't he, like, get caught with his teammate's girlfriend?" Roxy asks.

"No way. It was his teammate with *his* girlfriend," I say.

Roxy's and Jocelyn's eyes widen.

"Damn," Jocelyn says.

"Yeah. It was pretty fucked up. I only know that because he once mentioned it to Drew during guys' night and Drew told me," I say.

"Yeah, Bray said something similar," Carly agrees.

"Anyhoo, enough about the men in our building. We need to figure out how we can get intel on McDowell's," Roxy says.

Everyone is silent for a moment as we each consider the best way for me to go about finding details on what this new McDowell's will serve. I have given a lot of thought to ways to differentiate myself from them, but without knowing what they plan on doing, it's hard to predict. McDowell's is known for making each location unique. They aren't a cookie-cutter type of store, so the predictability isn't there.

"Hear me out," Jocelyn starts and we all turn to her. "What if...you sleep with him."

My eyes widen. "W-what?" I manage. Piper is sitting in the corner and she giggles.

Jocelyn waves her hands in a "simmer down" motion and speaks again. "Why not take the whole keep-your-enemies-closer thing all the way? There are so many great spy stories in history where women spies slept with men to get access to their secrets. So, what if you become a spy."

Sadly, she's not wrong about that. There are plenty of those stories on and off the big screen. I just don't think I could do it.

"I don't know," I say. "That seems...I don't think I could do it."

She frowns. "OK. What about just seducing him a little?"

Carly starts laughing. "What does *a little* mean?"

"Like, turn on the Cam charm. Make him think with his dick instead of his brain. Maybe he'll slip up and spill some secrets," Jocelyn says.

Roxy elbows her.

"Ouch! What was that for?" Jocelyn says, glaring at her boss and friend.

"You have got to stop reading mafia romance books," Roxy says with a roll of her eyes.

Jocelyn shrugs and pulls out her phone, typing away for a few seconds. "I mean, you have to admit. The man is hot as fuck," she says as she turns her phone around. Roxy swipes it from her hand and whistles.

"OK, yeah, maybe we revisit the sleeping-with-him thing," Roxy says as she looks at some photos of him.

"Not happening. He's a billionaire-heir playboy asshole. No way. I don't care..." I trail off as Roxy turns the phone around and I'm greeted by a photo of Fletcher McDowell in only his underwear. It's clearly a paparazzi photo. He's on a rooftop deck with earbuds in and a phone in his hand. But it's not his surroundings that draw my attention. Nope. That would be his perfect male physique and the enormous bulge in his gray boxer briefs.

"You were saying?" Jocelyn teases.

Carly leans forward and gulps. "I think you should take one for the team," she whispers in a breathy voice.

Roxy gives her a little shove.

"What? I mean...I know I haven't had any in a while but look at that man," she says as she glances over her shoulder at Roxy who just nods.

"Let me see," Margie insists as she holds out her hand. Jessa and Cornelia lean forward and the three of them all look at the photo as their eyes widen.

"Wow," Margie says after a beat.

"Wow? More like hubba hubba," Cornelia says. We all giggle at her words.

Jessa looks over at me. "What is your plan?"

I sigh and consider all the things I've thought about so far. "I think I need to call a truce, and then once I have his trust, I'll start asking about the new place, little by little until I get a better picture of what it will be. Then, I need to come up with my own marketing campaign and adjust bakery items and such."

"OK, how will you gain his trust? He's a playboy, but he's not stupid," Roxy says.

I nod. "I know. I—"

"Mom!" Ava yells out her window.

Carly pokes her head out of Margie and Cornelia's window. "Ava, so help me. Get your head back in your room right now."

"But, Mom, I need you to text Unca Bray and tell him I can have a second cookie," she whines.

"Ava, go brush your teeth. It's bedtime," Carly screams.

"But, Mom," she whines.

"Sorry, Carly. I got this," Bray's voice calls out.

"Do you? Because it does not sound like it," she says as she leans out the window and stares in the direction of her apartment.

"Yep, all is good. Someone is a little sour about no second cookie tonight," he replies.

"Yeah. Tell me about it. I'll be up in an hour," she says.

"Take your time," he replies.

Carly pops her head back into the apartment. And suddenly, I have an idea.

"I need to win over his family," I state.

"Huh?" Carly says in confusion as she sits back down.

"Think about it. We all trust each other because we're like family, right?" I start.

Everyone nods. "So, if I can win over his family, he's more likely to trust me."

Piper finally pipes up. "Project Infiltrate the McDowell Family starts now. We need a plan for you. These are billionaires. They aren't just going to trust any old person."

Everyone stares at Piper, mostly because she's got a point.

"What? I watch a lot of reality television shows with rich people," she says with a shrug.

"Alright, what's your plan, then?" I ask her and she grins as she rubs her hands together.

"We need to do some reconnaissance and I know just the

hacker to help us," she says with a grin and a wink as she motions to Kasen's apartment across the hall from this one. Dear God, what am I about to do?

CHAPTER TWELVE

Fletch

"Fuck, these are really good," Dalton practically moans as he finishes an eggnog cookie.

"Can we just get her to bake for our store?" Spencer asks.

I glare at my brothers. "First, she's our competitor. So no. And second, we get to keep these recipes. Remember?"

"Oh, right. It's in the contract," Spencer says smirking. I refrain from rolling my eyes. I love Spence but sometimes he is so focused on the forest he forgets he's surrounded by trees. Details are not his thing.

"You're an idiot," Dalton growls as he grabs another cookie and a cupcake.

"So what's the plan? This woman has culinary skills. Do we just sink obscene amounts of money into the Hearts Lane location? Do we search for a renowned pastry chef with a following on social media to run the bakery? Do we cut a special deal with some coffee suppliers for special beans?

What's the path forward?" Dalton continues as he takes a bite of the cupcake and his eyes roll back in his head. I hear the telltale pop of a candied cranberry and I shake my head.

"I don't know. I need to get more intel. If she's given us these recipes, then I know she has some way better things up her sleeve. She's not going to give away her best ideas," I point out.

"True. You need to spend time with her. Gain her trust, figure out her secrets, and then we pivot before opening with a new direction that can crush her store," Spencer says matter-of-factly.

"Exactly," I state.

Dalton laughs. "Why the hell would she trust *you?*"

"Because I'm witty and charming," I say with a smirk. Both my brothers double over with laughter and I flick them off. "Fuck you both. Women love me. I'll figure her out. Give me a few weeks."

The competition starts in another week. I've already scheduled time with her this week to go over our strategies and backup plans, but then as her team coordinator, I'll be intimately involved in every aspect of our team's baking. The competition calls for the bakers to have one assistant and she's already told me some woman at the bakery will be there. I just hope that doesn't screw up my plan to be able to gain her trust.

"Bro, you need to tread lightly with this one," Spencer adds as he takes a piece of the pie. He takes a bite and his eyes widen. "How did she even do that?"

I shrug. "We haven't gone over the process yet," I answer as I take a cookie.

Spencer types something on his phone and his eyes widen. "Wait a damn minute. This is the competition?" he asks as he flips his phone around to reveal a photo of Camryn.

I nod, forcing myself to swallow the cookie. Holy fuck-balls! It's a candid shot someone took as a promo piece on the café. She's throwing her head back and laughing. Her curly red hair is up high in a ponytail, but tendrils hang down around her face. She's gorgeous.

"I mean, maybe I can talk to her," Spencer says as he looks at the photo. I practically growl as I shove his phone back toward him. There is no fucking way I'm letting Spencer anywhere near Camryn. I might have the playboy reputation from the antics of my youth, but Spencer eats women for dinner and spits them out for dessert. He can never keep a girlfriend longer than three months. It's like he purposefully repels them once things start to get serious.

Dalton leans in to see what has us transfixed. He whistles. "She's beautiful," he says. Now, I'm angry. I feel like a feral dog ready to mark his territory.

"I have this under control. I can handle her," I say through gritted teeth.

Spencer laughs. "Right. We all know how you *handle* women," he says with a smirk. I want to punch that look right off his face.

I clench my fists at my sides. "I got this," I growl as I turn and walk out of the room before I do or say something I might regret.

I make it to my office and sit down, swiveling my chair to stare out at the city below. What the fuck just came over me? I'm not with Camryn. Who cares if Spencer or Dalton went after her? Why did I just feel protective of this woman who drives me insane?

My assistant's voice rings out from my desk phone and I welcome the distraction. I don't want to spend another second pondering why I just felt the overwhelming need to protect my biggest rival.

"OK," I say as I look around the kitchen. "What's first?"

It's Sunday evening and Camryn has invited me over to walk me through baking each item. We will be holed up at an estate just outside the city for the competition starting next weekend, so this is our last chance to go over things.

"I'm here," another voice calls out and an older woman walks into the room.

"This is Amber," Camryn says as she motions to the woman.

Amber reaches out and shakes my hand. "So, you're Fletcher," she says eyeing me up and down. I suddenly feel like I'm being judged and not in a good way.

"That would be me," I manage as I glance back over at Camryn. She's smirking and I glare at her. She shrugs and claps her hands together.

"Amber has worked in the kitchen here longer than I've worked here. She knows everything there is to know about baking," Camryn explains as she sets out bowls of ingredients.

She pats a stool to the side of a workbench and I sit.

"Good boy," she whispers and winks at me. I glare at her.

She grins, clearly loving that she got under my skin.

"Now, we are going to have to perfect the quantities this week because we need to make a small batch for the judges instead of the large batches we normally make. The pie will be easy enough, but for the cookies and cupcakes we'll need to pare down. Amber and I have worked out what seems to be the correct formula over the past few days. We will walk you through that tonight," she explains as she turns to Amber.

"Let's do the cupcakes first," she adds and Amber nods, bringing a tray of ingredients to the worktable. She talks me through her process first and then stops and looks over at me.

"Get your ass over here. You're going to help," she says.

I raise my eyebrows. She motions for me to stand next to her. Normally, I wouldn't cave to taking directions from this pint-sized rival of mine, but for reasons I can't explain, I listen to her.

She takes my hand in hers and wraps both our hands around a giant spoon in a bowl of dry ingredients. I hate admitting I like the feel of her hand on mine, but I'd be a fucking liar if I denied it.

"Stir," she commands as she moves our hand in a circle. "Good job," she says in a low voice before letting go of my hand.

The air feels cold against my skin where her hand had been, but I keep swirling the spoon in the bowl until she tells me to stop.

"OK, Amber has the wet ingredients going. We're going to start pouring the dry ingredients into that larger bowl," she says as she motions toward Amber's bowl. "Hold the bowl for me."

I do as I'm told and she uses a spatula to slowly incorporate the dry ingredients into the larger bowl.

Then she shows me how to make the candied cranberries and frosting while Amber fills the cupcake molds. We're all working seamlessly together. And finally, the cupcakes go in the oven.

"Now what?" I ask.

"Now, you're going to help me make cookies," she says and I groan. How did I forget we had two more baked goods to make?

She bumps me with her hip and I suddenly remember that I need to gain her trust. So I decide to be playful. I throw some flour from the table on her.

"You did not just do that?" she says as she brushes it off her chin.

"I did," I state.

She picks up some flour from a container and throws it on me.

"You guys!" Amber says loudly but it's too late. We're in a full food fight and I completely forget that I'm with my enemy.

CHAPTER THIRTEEN

Cam

I throw tampons into my suitcase as I try to remember what I might have forgotten. Tonight I get whisked away to the filming location for the bake-off. The network has decided it wants to make this a bigger deal than it was previously. So now, I'm calling in Phyllis to run the café while I film and I hired Amber's cousin, Stacey, to help out while Amber films with me. It's not ideal but it's only for three weeks.

As if I'm not already dealing with anxiety and nerves, my body had to throw in my period. Freaking fantastic.

I look around the room and then remember the missing saltshaker. I run into the kitchen and start tearing things apart. I want my good-luck saltshaker with me. It's my good-luck charm. Every time I've nailed a recipe, I've had it sitting on the counter. I don't know if it's because it's so entwined with my first memory of baking or if I've developed an unhealthy obsession, but either way, I want it with me.

My phone pings with a text from my brother. I realize we haven't talked in days.

Winston: Good luck! I'm sure you'll win.

Me: Thanks! Fingers crossed.

I soon get good-luck texts from both my parents. I swear the three of them have some group chat about me.

Then I see a message from Max.

Max: Didn't you say you had some big thing for work this week? If so, best of luck and I hope it turns out well.

He remembered. I smile goofily at his message. God, I wish he was dating material. He's a really good person.

Me: Thanks! I do and I'm super nervous.

I haven't given Max details because that violates our conversation rules but it's sweet of him to remember something important was happening.

Max: Just be yourself.

Me: LOL!

Max: I am serious.

Me: Uh, OK. But being myself can be...a lot.

Max: The world deserves to see the real E.

Me: Thanks (blushing emoji)

I toss my phone on the counter and rifle through the cabinets. I start pulling things out as anxiety creeps in. What am I doing?

I sit back against a cupboard door and close my eyes, willing the threatening tears away but they come anyhow. I feel them, big and fat, rolling down my cheeks. What if I fail? What if all of these past years' hard work was for nothing?

I want to make my family proud. I want to prove I can do this, that I'm not a little girl who speaks before she thinks, not anymore.

I wish my grandmother was here. I'm sure she'd have something brilliant to say.

I let the tears come harder as I sob under the pressure of

it all. I have employees who need me to be strong and here I am crying on my kitchen floor.

I pull my knees to my chest and let my forehead fall to them as I wrap my arms around my legs. I don't know how long I'm here for, but suddenly I hear my front door open.

Shit. Drew.

I swipe at the tears on my cheeks as I start shoving things back into the cupboards.

"I'm just grabbing a few more things and then I'm heading out," I say loudly hoping my voice doesn't give away the complete breakdown I just had.

"Camryn?" a very familiar deep voice says as its owner rounds the corner.

My head whips around to look at none other than Mr. Fletcher McDowell.

What. In. The. Fuck?

He takes one look at me and then steps into the kitchen in half the strides it should take. He glances around us, his eyes looking me up and down. "Hey, what's wrong?" he asks, his voice surprisingly soft, a look of concern on his face.

I swallow a lump that just re-formed in the back of my throat. Why is he suddenly being so kind? I can deal with asshole Fletcher. I can deal with businessman Fletcher. I can even deal with annoying, spying Fletcher. But this...kind and concerned Fletcher. Nope. I can't do it.

"Nothing," I mutter as I turn and take the pepper shaker from my counter. It's not the same, but it will have to do. "I'm almost packed."

I step around him but he grabs my upper arm.

"Are you OK?" he asks.

I rip my arm from his grasp. "Of course, I am." I pause as I head to my bedroom. "How'd you get in here?"

"Al let me in. I saw him in the hallway and said I was picking you up for the competition. I knocked but you didn't answer." Great. I probably couldn't hear it over my sobbing. Fuck. I am such a mess. "He had the master key on him. So he let me in to make sure you were alright. I'll let him know you are." He pulls out his phone and types a message, presumably to Al.

"I'll just be a minute," I state as I practically run into my room and finish packing in record time.

I hear a knock at my window and I look out to see…a donkey on a stick? The donkey is tapping at my window. I rub my eyes. Clearly, I've reached the state where I am just hallucinating. Yep, that's it.

What the hell is happening?

I walk to my window and open it, looking forward at the donkey and then down.

"Oh, good. It reached your window," Ava says.

I frown. "Ava, what the hell are you doing?"

"Sending you Mr. Pickles," she says as she pushes the… long pole further out of her window, or should I say her mother's window.

"Ava," I hiss. "You are going to fall. Stop. And what is happening here?"

"Bray won't let me leave to give you Mr. Pickles, so I borrowed this lightbulb changer thing that Mr. Troy left in the hallway. It's how he changes the lightbulbs in the ceiling," she explains.

I slap my forehead. For the love of God.

"Ava! Will you stop hanging out of windows? It's danger-ous," I state, my sadness of several minutes ago quickly evap-orating as fears for this child's safety take center stage in my brain.

"Why does everyone always say that?" she asks, her face twisted up in true puzzlement.

"And this is why I don't have kids," I mutter to myself.

"Huh?" she asks.

"Nothing. I think you should keep Mr. Pickles," I announce.

"Oh come on. You can put him on TV and he'll be famous!" she says excitedly.

"Won't you miss him? I'll be gone for three weeks," I explain and I feel a presence in my room. I turn to see Fletcher standing in the doorway. His gaze darts between me and the stuffed donkey hanging in front of me. Great. My room is in its normal messy state. I'm sure discarded underwear lies somewhere around here. But I don't have time to process my mortification as Ava speaks again.

"Nope. I'm a big kid now. I don't need stuffed animals," she explains proudly.

"Fine. But if you get upset about him being gone for so long, I don't want to hear about it," I grumble.

"I won't," she assures me with a big grin.

I reach out to grab the donkey and my foot slips on a T-shirt I may have left on my floor. I grip the window ledge but start to double over and I feel my feet leave the ground.

Suddenly, strong arms wrap around my middle.

"Whoa," Fletcher says into my ear. He tightens his grip on me as he sets me back down. Then he reaches past me and un-tapes the donkey from the stick, and hands it to me. His front is flush with my back, his hands are on either side of me and I feel his breath against my hair.

"Who are you?" Ava asks.

"I'm going to be your worst nightmare if you don't stick yourself back into your apartment," he growls.

I lean over a little and see Ava's eyes widen. "Ava, we got Mr. Pickles. Mr. Fletcher here is my...uh...work colleague. We have to go. I'll see you in a few weeks. Please, behave."

Ava giggles. "I always behave, silly goose." I hear Bray's voice and Ava quickly pulls the long pole down. "Gotta go. Bye," she says quickly and disappears.

I realize Fletcher is gripping my hip as if afraid I'll tumble over the window ledge. I have nowhere to step, so I lean back into him and hold up the donkey.

"I think we have a mascot," I say dryly.

"Uh, can we wash him?" he asks.

I tilt my head to look up at him and he looks down at me. "Do you think he'd survive that?"

Fletcher grimaces. "Probably not."

"Then, no. Mr. Pickles is coming as is," I say as I look back at the stuffed animal. My phone pings in my pocket and I pull it out to see a message from Al.

Al: I hope you don't mind. I let Fletcher in.

I sigh and I feel Fletcher's neck crane to read my text. I don't have to turn to know the jackass is smirking.

Me: It's fine.

I lie. What was Al thinking? I decide to yell at him over drinks when I get back. I don't have time right now.

The front door opens and Fletcher steps away from me.

"Honey! I'm home," Drew's voice echoes throughout the apartment.

I turn to see Fletcher raising one eyebrow.

Drew appears in my doorway and the look of surprise is so good, I almost want to take a photo.

"Oh, I, uh, didn't know you had company," he says and his facial features start morphing into a knowing look. Fuck my life.

"I don't. I mean, he's not my guest. I mean, we're just leaving," I stammer as I try to form a sentence.

Fletcher suddenly finds his manners and walks over to Drew, holding out his hand. "Fletcher," he introduces himself.

Drew shakes it and then glances over Fletcher's shoulder at me. I roll my eyes and he smirks.

"So, how's it feel to be the neighborhood jackass?" he asks Fletcher.

Fletcher's moving arm stops and Drew steps back.

"I didn't know such a title existed," Fletcher grumbles.

"Oh, it does and you are it. Best of luck opening your store," he says and looks back at me. "Good luck, Camelot. You got this," he adds with a wink. I groan. I hate it when he uses old nicknames.

Fletcher turns and I can tell he loves that Drew just let slip a nickname. I want to murder both of them but I don't have time.

"OK, then, let's go," I urge as I stuff Mr. Pickles into a bag I find lying on a chair and then grab my suitcase and over-sized purse.

"You're wearing that?" Fletcher asks as he looks at me. I'm in jean shorts and a T-shirt because I was planning to change for the opening meeting after we get settled at this place where we're staying.

"Yep," I state not explaining anymore because I'm annoyed and also want Fletcher to sweat a little.

He sighs and takes my suitcase from me. "Fine. Let's go. Nice meeting you…Darryl?" he says to Drew.

Drew glares at him. "Drew," he corrects.

"Right. Nice meeting you, Drew," Fletcher says, drawing out Drew's name. I watch the two of them do some sort of male testosterone standoff and I roll my eyes.

I grab Fletcher's forearm and yank on it. "Let's go."

He starts moving and I give Drew a pointed look. Drew gives me a look that says, "What is going on?"

I shrug because honestly, I am still processing Mr. Pickles, Ava, and Fletcher saving my life.

I walk out the door and start down the stairs.

"Are we not taking the elevator?" he asks as he motions to it.

"Do you value your life?" I reply.

"Oh, not working?" he says.

"Let's just say it breaks down enough that unless I'm forced to take it, I don't," I explain as I walk down the stairs, careful to hold on to the railing because I don't need Fletcher rescuing me again. It feels like I owe him something and I don't like owing people anything.

I hear Margie in the entryway as we round the staircase.

"And then he said everyone is doing it and I couldn't believe that. When was the last time you did it in the ass?" she asks someone.

"Oh? Really?" Her voice is so loud that I'm fairly certain she is talking to someone on the phone who is hard of hearing.

"Wow. OK. I'll pass that on to Cornelia too. Good to know," she says as she comes into my view. She's at the mailboxes and on the phone. She has her cell phone up to her ear.

"Great. We'll have to grab coffee next week. Yep. Talk to you later," she says as she turns and smiles at me. "Off to the competition?"

I nod. "Yep. Heading there now."

She walks over and hugs me. "Well, good luck," she says, completely oblivious to the fact that we just overhead her ass discussion.

"Thanks," I manage as I fight back a laugh.

"Who's this fine young man?" she asks as she steps back.

Oh dear God! Can the earth swallow me up now?

"This would be Fletcher McDowell," I state. "Fletcher, this is my neighbor Margie."

"Nice to meet you," he says, offering his free hand.

She shakes it while narrowing her eyes and then pulls back her hand and points it at his chest. "You better watch it, young man. Our Camryn will be winning that competition and her café is the best in the city. Everyone knows it. Your little store doesn't stand a chance."

"Right. Thanks for the warning?" he says but it comes out as a question.

"Consider yourself warned," she adds. And then waves and smiles as she goes into the elevator.

"I thought you said..." He trails off as he points to the elevator.

I groan. "Let's just pretend we didn't hear any of that and Margie doesn't care about getting stuck. She's retired and has more time than sense."

"Oh," is all he says as we walk out the door to a waiting limo. His hand goes to the small of my back as we approach the car. It's a little thing. I'm sure he'd do it out of politeness for any woman as she gets in a car but something about it feels...intimate.

I take a deep breath as the driver opens the door for us and takes the luggage. Here goes nothing.

CHAPTER FOURTEEN

Fletch

My mind is going a million miles a minute as we drive out of the city. I have thousands of questions about Camryn's roommate, her neighbors, and her. She was definitely crying when I arrived. I felt such an overwhelming need to comfort her. I have no idea why and I can't think about that right now. I need to focus.

Glancing over, I study Camryn. She's looking out the window. Her eyes aren't glazed over like before but she looks deep in thought.

"Everything alright?" I ask again. I tell myself that I'm asking because I need her to make our company look good in this competition. But that's a lie, a lie I'm not willing to explore.

Fuck, what the hell is wrong with me?

She looks back over at me, her eyes searching mine. "I'm fine. Just...mentally preparing," she says as she gives me a small smile, but it doesn't reach her eyes and I know she's lying.

I nod. The driver pulls off the main road onto a long tree-lined drive. I've been to events out at this estate before but it's been years. As the manor house comes into view, I'm reminded of how impressive it is. I glance over and see Camryn's eyes widen. I fight a smile at her innocent reaction to the size of the dwelling. It was built by a wealthy family in the early nineteen hundreds. There are gardens, a gatekeeper's house, a groundskeeper's cottage, stables, and a dozen other little outbuildings on fifty acres. But it's the main house that's impressive as hell. Built from reclaimed buildings abroad, it's in the Tudor style of an English manor house. Its steep roof pitches and stonework remind me of places I've stayed in the English countryside. The competition itself will take place in climate-controlled tents in the back gardens of the property.

We come to a stop and the driver gets out and opens the car doors for us. Camryn stands perfectly still as I walk around the car. There's a bustle of activity around us as staff take luggage and offer us drinks. Camryn takes a flute of champagne with only a simple "thank you."

I'm about to ask her again if she's alright but an older woman approaches us.

"Camryn Tanner?" she asks.

Camryn nods.

The woman holds out her hand. "I'm Felicity Centric, the producer for the show. I'm going to get you settled." Felicity looks around. "Where's Amber?"

"Oh, she said she needed to check in on her mother and she'd drive separately," Camryn explains.

"OK. Well, we'll get you two set up now and I'll meet Amber later, then," Felicity says as she claps her hands and motions for us to follow her.

We walk inside into the grand foyer. "We've put your team in the Lexington Suite upstairs. I hope that's fine," she says as we follow her up the staircase and down a hall.

"Sure," Camryn says as we approach large double doors. Felicity takes out a key card and opens them. They have clearly been added more recently. The hallway continues past them with a couple of bedrooms with en suites and a large living area at the end of the hall.

"This is all your suite. I put you and Amber in here," she says as she motions to a door, and Camryn peeks inside. It's a large suite with two queen beds and a sitting area. "And you're over here, Mr. McDowell." She motions across the hall to a large king-bed suite. "The Wi-Fi passwords and information about the competition with times and locations are in your welcome packets. We have a reception in the great hall tonight at seven after dinner. Dinner will be served at six in the formal dining room. Any questions?"

"Nope," Camryn says as she takes her suite key from Felicity.

"I think we're good. Thank you, Felicity," I say as I accept a key.

"Wonderful. I'll see you both at dinner," she says as she leaves us standing in the hallway. I look past Camryn to see her luggage has already been set out in her room.

"Well, I...uh...I guess we should get settled," I suggest because staring at the bed behind her has my mind concocting impossible situations that it should not. My gaze goes back to her, but instead of looking directly into her eyes, I note that her sweater has slipped to one side, exposing the black strap of her bra. Fuck. I need to get my mind out of the gutter.

I clear my throat and force myself to look into her eyes. She's watching me with a mild smirk on her lips. Damn it. I've been caught ogling her.

I look down at the packet I snatched off my bed while she was talking to Felicity and I pull out the papers. The top one is the agenda for this weekend.

"It's business casual for dinner this evening," is all I manage to say as I turn to go into my bedroom. I don't look back as I close the door and lean back against it. This is going to be the most trying three weeks of my life.

I decide to spend most of the next hour catching up on work. I have change orders to approve and a quick video chat with our general contractor. By the time I finish, it's five twenty. I hear a shower turn off and then a blood-curdling scream.

I jump out of my seat and run across the hallway, throwing open Camryn's bedroom door and looking around wildly.

"Camryn!" I call out as I scan my surroundings. I run toward the bathroom when I don't see her in the bedroom. Flinging the door open, I come face to face with a half-naked Camryn. A towel is wrapped around her body but barely. Her hair is wet and she's standing on the toilet making her taller than me by a few inches.

"What in the..." I trail off as I try to figure out what the hell is going on in here.

"S-spider," she stammers as she points to a small spider in the corner of the room.

I look back at her with a raised eyebrow and point to it. "That is the reason for...this," I say as I motion to her on the toilet.

She nods. Her eyes are wide and her face is flushed. She's legitimately scared.

I suddenly envision dumping hundreds of spiders in her café. I didn't think getting rid of it would be so easy. I shake my head at the ridiculous thought.

"How do you function in the real world?" I ask her as I bend down and scoop the spider on my hand.

"Oh, God! Get it away!" she screeches as she tries to crawl anywhere, which ends up being on the counter of the sink.

I groan in frustration at her reaction. I take the spider to the small balcony off her room and let it go into some ivy that's growing along the bricks.

"There you go. Wouldn't want you scaring our star contestant, now would we?" I say to it with a roll of my eyes.

I walk back inside to find Camryn still crouched on the sink. Her shapely legs are exposed and her breasts are almost popping out of the top of the towel.

"I-is it gone?" she asks as she clutches at the towel.

"Yes," I answer, standing in front of her.

Her phone begins to ring and her gaze darts to the bed.

"Can you..." She trails off and points to the bed, clearly wanting me to get her phone for her.

"You can't be serious?" I give her a pointed look.

"I'm dead serious," she says, her fiery anger starting to take over now that the fear is subsiding.

"Camryn, don't be ridiculous. The spider is gone. You're fine," I state dryly as I step to the side to allow her to get down. She looks around and I know she can't figure out how to get off the sink.

I hold out a hand to help her down.

"Cover your eyes," she insists.

I sigh and close my eyes.

"Are your eyes closed all the way?" she asks.

"Yes," I grumble.

I feel her hand slide into mine and a moment later her body weight tugs at my arm as she jumps down. She falters slightly and I pull her against me to steady her.

It's at the moment of contact that I realize her towel has slipped loose because I feel her naked breasts pressed against my thin button-down shirt. Holy hell! I feel my body begin to react and I don't want her to know that she affects me like that. I move my hips back slightly so I'm not pressing my hardening dick against her abdomen.

"Shit," she squeaks, and her hands start moving, probably to get the towel, but if anything, I'm true to my word, and against every desire I have, I don't peek.

She steps away. "You can open your eyes now," she says, and I open them to find her standing a foot away, the towel wrapped around her once again.

"Are we better now?" I ask, masking my desire with sarcasm.

This time, it's Camryn rolling her eyes. "Yes," she huffs. Her cheeks are pink and her chest is flushed in the same color. Part of me wonders if I have any effect on her or if it's just me who has inappropriate thoughts.

"Good. I'm going to send a few more emails before dinner," I state as I walk past her, getting a whiff of honeysuckle. I need to get out of here before I do something stupid.

"Thanks," she calls out meekly as I leave her room. I wave my hand in the air and leave without another word or look because I don't trust myself around her, especially not when she's nearly naked. How I'm going to survive the next three weeks, I have no idea.

CHAPTER FIFTEEN

Cam

I stand out on the balcony off my bedroom. I'm mortified by what just happened. He nearly saw me naked. And if I'm being honest with myself, I'm more mortified that I liked how his body felt wrapped around mine. Images of his strong hands holding my hips while I grind down on him danced across my mind for long seconds as we stood in my bathroom with my naked breasts pressed to his chest and his arms wrapped tightly around me. I hate that I liked the way it felt. I hate that he has these sweet moments that make me like him. I'm so confused. I should just hate this man. It should be easy to hate him, but for some reason, it's becoming harder and harder. I have no idea what to do.

I've called everyone I know trying to get advice, but of course, they are all busy. So I've resorted to messaging Max. I wish I could just give him details. It'd make life so much easier.

Me: I need advice.

It takes a minute but then I see three dots indicating he's replying. I sit down on one of the two chairs on the balcony.

Max: What's up?

Me: What would you do if you found yourself attracted to someone who you shouldn't be attracted to?

I expect to see those three dots appear right away because Max is great with life advice, but there's nothing. Several minutes pass and I'm about to give up on waiting and go finish touching up my hair when I see he's replying.

Max: Entertainingly, I'm in the same boat, so I have no advice for you, only empathy.

Me: Seriously! LOL! What should we do?

Max: No idea. (shrugging emoji)

Me: Wow! Proper use of emojis! Look at you!

Max: (middle-finger emoji)

I smile. I feel the slightest bit better.

Max: Maybe we try to be friends with the person? Maybe they aren't as bad as we thought.

Me: That's too adult of us. (laughing emoji)

Max: It might be.

Me: Sigh. I hate being the bigger person.

Max: Same.

Me: Fine. But we have to promise to check back in with each other in a few days to reassess our idea.

Max: A debrief. Done.

Me: Good luck. May the force be with you.

Max: And with you.

I laugh and put my phone away. I glance at my watch and realize the time. Where's Amber?

I pull my phone out as I walk back to the bathroom to check my hair one last time. And see I've missed a call from her. Huh? When did Amber call?

I call her back.

"Oh, thank goodness. I feel so bad. My mom is not doing

well and the doctor wants me to take her to the emergency room. I definitely won't be there tonight, but depending on what happens, I may not be there at all," she says, her words coming out rushed. I can hear the telltale sounds of the hospital in the background, the beeping machines, the rolling of carts and beds, and nurses and doctors talking in medical lingo that reminds me of Bray.

"Is Bray there?" I ask.

"He doesn't come on for another hour, but I texted him," Amber replies.

"Good. I'll feel better if he's there to assess your mom. And don't worry. I'll figure it out. You take care of your mom and let me know if you need anything," I say.

"Thanks, Cam. I really am sorry about all of this. It's horrible timing," she says.

"No worries. Friends and family are always more impor-tant than business," I stress as I adjust my hair and walk out of my room.

"Thanks. I'll let you know what they say," she adds.

"OK. Good luck," I say as I hang up and look across the hall. Fletcher's door is open and he's typing on his computer. He looks every part the serious businessman. I study him for a moment, not wanting to interrupt his work. He really is very handsome. His dark, messy hair falls over his hazel eyes. His jaw tics as his eyes scan something. He moves his arm and his bicep flexes, pulling his shirt tight against it. The man definitely is in shape. I can see how women would fall at his feet. He's smart and gorgeous. Too bad he can be such a jerk. If he wasn't so freaking irritating...then there's that little issue of his company trying to put mine out of business.

With a heavy sigh, I lean on his doorjamb. "Ready?" I ask.

He looks up quickly and then back at his computer and then back at me. His eyebrows rise slightly. "You clean up well, Tanner," he says as his eyes peruse my body.

I'm not sure why I feel more naked than I did a few minutes ago when he saw me in only a towel, but somehow I do.

I cross my arms over my breasts because the look he's giving me makes me feel not only naked but also exposed as if he can see inside my head to my most personal thoughts.

"I'm heading down," I state, turning to grab my key from the side table in the main hallway of the suite.

"Wait up," he says and I hear him get up. A second later he's next to me.

We walk to the door, and when he opens it, he looks around us. "I thought Amber was meeting us here?"

Shit, how did I already forget that. One minute of staring at the man and I forget all the important things. "So...small pickle. Her mom has to go to the emergency room. She won't know more until the doctors check her. But...uh, yeah," I say as we begin walking.

He grabs my arm and pulls me into a small alcove in the hallway. "What?" he hisses.

I let out a long breath. "Amber is out for tonight. I won't know more until later tonight. I can text Adriana. She's new but she knows some things. If not, I guess I'm doing this solo," I explain with a frown as I realize what I'm saying. Ugh. I'm going to have to tell Felicity this.

"What?" he says loudly this time.

"You heard me," I say, my voice rising.

"We can't compete if you have no assistant. Every other team has two people because the competition is for a *team*," he says, emphasizing the last word.

"I know that," I mutter.

"We'll figure this out after dinner. I'm sure I can get one of our pastry chefs to help," he says matter-of-factly.

I roll my eyes. "We'll cross that bridge later if we need to.

No sense worrying about something that might not even be an issue."

"You know what makes my family's company successful?" he asks as we begin walking again.

I don't answer but glance over at him.

He continues. "We constantly are planning for every scenario so when things go awry, and they always do, we're prepared and not scrambling last minute. You should have had a second person ready to go," he says sternly.

I stop and he turns to me. Jabbing a finger in his well-muscled chest, I glare up at him. "You can't plan your way out of every bump in the road that life has to offer. You have to be ready to work through them. And I'm ready. I can do this solo if I have to. I'll let Felicity know," I say, my shoulders sagging a little.

"No. Not yet. Let's wait to see what happens. We can tell her there was a family emergency and we're waiting to hear. That's it," he says angrily as we continue down the stairs and into the dining room.

The other three teams are all standing around. Cameras are rolling and the next two hours are a flurry of introductions, food, drinks, explanations, and awkward small talk. Two of the teams are from bakeries on the other side of the city. One specializes in cakes and the other in cookies. The third team is more similar to my store. They serve coffee and a variety of baked goods. Their number one selling item is their cupcakes, which they also sell online. All three teams have been around much longer than I have. Their businesses are larger and more reputable than mine. By the end of the meal, I already know that my store is the underdog contestant or at least that's what the show wants to pigeonhole me as. The only thing keeping me calm is my slight buzz from the three glasses of wine I've had.

It's as we are opening the suite door that I get the call

from Amber. I put it on speaker and look up at Fletcher, who has been quiet during the meal. He spoke a bit with the other sponsors but otherwise seemed very busy on his phone.

"Hey," she says and I know immediately it's not good.

"How bad is it?" I ask.

"Bad. She's going to need surgery. Her gallbladder has a stone that could cause a major issue. It's what is causing her pain. They want to do it first thing tomorrow and then she'll need me to stay with her for two weeks. I'm so sorry, Cam," she says and I can hear how tired she is. I want to be mad, but I don't have the energy and I know it's not her fault.

"It's alright, Amber. We'll figure it out. Go take care of your mom," I assure her.

"I will. Please let me know if there's anything I can do," she adds before we hang up.

I text Adriana without even looking at Fletcher.

Me: Any chance you could join me at the competition? Amber's mom is in the hospital.

Adriana: Oh no! I'm so sorry but I can't. Remember I told you that my brother might be able to visit. He flies in tomorrow. I was going to try to take off one day next week to spend with him.

Shit. She's been homesick for her family for weeks. I can't do that to her.

Me: No worries. I'll figure it out.

I finally look up at Fletcher. "I'm solo," I announce.

His phone buzzes with a text and he looks down at it. "Fuck," he mutters. "None of my bakers are available for three weeks. We'd have to fly someone in and the earliest they can be here is in ten days."

I chew on the inside of my cheek as I think. Then something pops into my memory. When everyone was scouring the internet for information on Fletcher, there was an article.

An article about a little boy who won a baking competition with his grandmother.

I look up into Fletcher's eyes. "What if...you did it?" I ask, my voice coming out more breathy than I like. I sound desperate.

I swallow hard as I watch a myriad of emotions play out over his face. Confusion. Skepticism. Annoyance.

"You won a competition as a kid," I point out.

Now he's frowning. "How'd you know that?" he asks.

I roll my eyes. "There's this thing called the internet," I state with a deadpan face.

"That was years ago," he says. "I...I was just a kid. Mostly that was my grandmother."

For the first time since we met, I see something I never thought I'd see on Fletcher's face. Vulnerability.

I put a hand on his shoulder and squeeze it. His eyes go from the ground to my face. "But you helped her. You could help me. Please. You're right. Those other teams are good. I need an assistant. I'd ask my neighbors but none of them bake. Not enough to help me. Drew is the closest one to being helpful but he can't take off for three weeks."

I watch Fletcher as he considers what I'm saying. "Please," I beg. Now it's me that feels vulnerable. This man can ruin me. Right now.

He turns and runs a hand through his hair. And slowly he turns back to me.

"OK," he says.

I release a breath that I didn't know I was holding.

"OK?" I repeat.

He nods. "OK," he says again. Then puts up a hand. "But no being obnoxious. And if I'm doing this, then...fuck it, we're winning this shit. We'll figure everything else out afterward," he says and then gives a small shake of his head as if he can hardly believe his own words.

A smile threatens on my face and I finally give in to it. I throw my hands around his neck and hug him. He doesn't move for a second and then I feel his arms come around me.

"You're a pain in my ass. You know that, Tanner," he says.

I giggle. "You haven't seen anything yet, McDowell," I reply as I let go and stand back from him. We both stand there smiling at each other. And for reasons I will never understand, I lean up and kiss him. Just a quick kiss. A thank-you kiss. Or at least, that's what I tell myself as I turn and walk into my room, shutting the door behind me and leaving a very stunned Fletcher standing in the hallway.

CHAPTER SIXTEEN

Fletch

I stand in front of the mirror as I shave. What in the hell happened last night? I can't believe she kissed me. Yes, it was a quick kiss. Yes, we both had a few glasses of wine. And yes, she was in the moment. But something about it felt...right.

"Fuck," I mutter to myself as I rinse my razor and set it down on a towel to dry. I walk back into the bedroom and pull a fresh suit from the closet but then I remember what transpired yesterday. I'm going to be on the front lines not standing off camera. Shit. I don't have anything to wear.

I pick up my phone and call my assistant.

Dana answers on the first ring.

"Everything alright?" she asks.

"Not really. I need a favor. I'm sending you a list of clothing. Can you please go get it from my apartment and then have it delivered to me?" I ask.

"Oh, uh, sure," she says. I always get the distinct feeling

that she feels like she's my babysitter, and to be fair, for a long time, she basically was.

"Great. Thanks, Dana," I state as I disconnect. The last thing I need is for her to tell my brothers' assistants and then they tell my brothers and pretty soon the entire family knows I'll be playing a baking assistant on television. This is not going as planned.

I sit down and look around. I did bring one pair of khakis and a polo shirt. I guess that will have to do for this morning.

I get dressed and walk out into the hallway. It's quiet. Too quiet. I knock on the door. Still no answer. I open the door and peek inside.

"Camryn?" I ask. I hear a sniffle and I walk into the room to find her sitting on a bed holding...well, I'm not entirely sure. It's a small telephone-shaped thing.

She looks up and wipes a tear from her cheek.

"Hey, what's wrong?" I ask. I rush over to her, kneeling so we are face to face.

"It's missing," she manages after a moment, pointing to the item in her right hand.

"What's missing?" I ask, looking around as if something will magically appear.

She lets out a shaky breath. "My grandmother's saltshaker," she explains as she holds up the item in her hand. I can now see it's a pepper shaker. There must be a set.

I look around the room. "Did you forget to pack it?"

She shakes her head. "It's what I was looking for the other night when you came by the apartment," she explains, wiping another stray tear. "It's like...my lucky charm. I was using it to bake a cake when I got the news that my small business loan was accepted. I had it when I got accepted to the culinary program at my college. I had it when I got my apartment lease signed. I've had it for all these milestones. It's...like she's here with me."

More tears fall and it breaks my heart. I wipe one away from her cheek with the back of my finger and she blushes.

"I'm sorry. I know this is crazy. I'm being crazy." She takes a steadying breath and sets the pepper shaker down on the mattress. Standing, she brushes invisible lint away from her pants. "Let's go. I need to get things set up and walk you through what Amber was going to do."

Shit. I nearly forgot about that. Suddenly, I'm nervous and I'm never nervous. I watch as Camryn walks into her bathroom and puts on some makeup and then stares at herself for a long moment.

I see a resilience in her. She's putting on a literal mask in the form of makeup. She's much stronger than I gave her credit.

"Let's go," she says. I follow her out of her room. Part of me wants to discuss last night's kiss. Another part of me wants to talk more about this missing saltshaker. But I decide, for now, that we need to concentrate on getting our station set up for this competition.

"Great. You're here. That's your station," Felicity says excitedly as we walk into the makeshift tent filled with four baking stations. There are several cameras set up for filming and the space is abuzz with activity. Camryn and I greet our competitors who are also filing in and starting to sort out their spaces.

We get to ours and Camryn stands in the middle of it with her hands on her hips. She reaches into her pocket as if to look for something and then gives a small shake of her head and pulls her hand free. I furrow my brows in confusion but don't have time to think more about it as she begins to go over our setup with me.

"Are you paying attention?" she asks as she points to a stack of muffin tins. I nod.

She rolls her eyes and repeats something about where I'll

be standing as we make the cupcakes. The reality of what we are about to do settles over me as she walks me through the process for each of our baked goods. I've seen it all in her kitchen at the café, but this feels different.

When she finishes, she looks around us and then up at me. "You ready?" she asks.

"As ready as I'll ever be," I mutter as I stand at my workstation, hands on the counter, as I survey the other teams. My brothers will never let me live this down. And, of course, it has to be televised.

I'm surprised when she places her hand on mine. I look down at where her fingers touch mine. Her skin is smooth and warm and something about it reassures me. My gaze finds hers.

"We got this," she whispers, giving me a hopeful smile. I can't help but return it. She's not wrong. I may not be a baker, but I've been in enough of our kitchens over the years to know some things about baking. Dad made each of us do an internship at a store when we were in college. And then there's Camryn. She's amazing. She moves around a kitchen as if she was made to operate one. But there's something more to it. It's not just her professionalism and baking skills. She loves it. She comes alive when she's in the kitchen. A small part of me is looking forward to this competition because I'm going to get to see her in her element and I think I'll be witnessing true genius at work. It's no longer about being rivals. Not for now at least.

———

"That was fun," Camryn says as we finish cleaning our station. Today was a practice day. We got to run through our first recipe. There was some filming done. Cam is a natural on camera. She acted as if she was a regular on a cooking show.

The next two days will be filming the first episode which means we will have our cookie competition. Then we have a day to reset and then a press day where they also bring in ticketed members of the public to try the different cookies. We get a day off and then we start on the next round of the competition. The last few days are an open house of sorts where the public gets to try all of our baked goods. And then the finale will be judged for the television production.

"It was," I say.

She bumps my hip. "Don't look so surprised," she laughs as she tosses a towel down on the counter.

I chuckle. "Fine. I was a little surprised. I didn't think this would be fun," I admit. "And I didn't know you'd be such a natural on camera, Hollywood," I add, giving her hip a playful bump.

She shrugs. "It was fun."

We bid goodbyes to our competitor teams who are all still cleaning. As we walk back to the main house, she looks over at me. "You know your way around a kitchen," she states.

I nod.

"How?"

I smirk. "Don't look so shocked," I say.

She groans. "Are you going to tell me or not? You already said you didn't have that many skills from the competition you did with your grandmother when you were little."

I clear my throat and open the side door to the manor house. She steps through but glances up at me with curiosity as she does. Part of me still isn't sure I can trust her. Should I give her any personal information? Hell, why not? This life detail doesn't really matter and half of my life is already splashed all over the internet, which I'm sure she's seen.

"I spent a summer interning with one of our chefs," I explain.

"Seriously?" she asks as we walk upstairs.

"Yep. François was...a tyrant in the kitchen," I say with a laugh as I remember his antics.

"Damn. François Leroy?" she asks.

I nod. He's a very renowned baker who had a show on a food channel. My father offered him money he couldn't refuse and he took over our Paris bakery. He also made a training program for several of our other flagship stores.

"The very one. He was merciless," I admit.

She giggles. "I can only imagine. His reputation precedes him," she says.

I unlock our suite door and she steps inside. I watch her release a long breath and I wonder what she's thinking.

"I'm going to take a shower before dinner. See you down there?" she says as she opens her bedroom door.

"Sure. I need to do the same. I think I have flour in places it shouldn't be," I say with a chuckle.

She pauses and turns back to me, a wide grin on her face. "You surprised me today, Fletcher. I don't surprise easily," she confesses.

I shrug. "I suppose I'm the king of exceeding people's expectations."

She frowns. "Why's that?"

"When they don't think you have any capabilities, you tend to shock them," I explain as I recall all the times people thought I was just a spoiled, playboy jerk who couldn't do anything because he walked around with a silver spoon in his mouth.

Her frown deepens. "I didn't mean to insult you like that." Her lips twitch a little as if she's fighting a smirk. "I mean, under normal circumstances, I would, but since we're...in a truce and all..." She trails off with a shrug but I see a look of concern in her eyes and that surprises me. There's no way Camryn Tanner would care about me. Is there?

"Go shower," I command and I shut the door to my room.

Pulling out my phone, I decide I need to try to help her. No, I want to help her. Fuck. What is she doing to me?

"Al?" I answer when he picks up.

"Fletch?" he says.

"I need a favor," I start. "We have a missing saltshaker situation."

CHAPTER SEVENTEEN

Cam

I'm feeling calm this morning as I get dressed. Yesterday surprised me. Hell, really, it was Fletcher that surprised me. He's not the monster I thought he was and I'm not sure how I feel about that. Or maybe he is and I'm being fooled. I don't know which way is up. I feel like I've fallen down some crazy rabbit hole and the universe is upside down.

I check my phone and there's a message from the apartment group chat and Max. I check the one from Max first.

Max: Good luck with your business endeavor today. Hope it goes well!

I smile and check the group chat.

Drew: If those judges don't vote for you, I'm coming out there and kicking some asses.

Al: They'll win. I know it.

Margie: Good luck from Cornelia and me!

Carly: Don't kill your assistant and good luck!

I grin.

Roxy: Good luck from everyone at the bookstore and Gray. He's in a sound studio all day.

Bray: The emergency room says good luck!

I giggle.

Troy: Jessa and I wanted to say good luck too!

Kasen: I know how to take down a studio production's web access if you need me to.

Piper: Kasen! Don't listen to him! Good luck!

I shake my head.

Hutch: (photo of flowers on the bench) Today's flowers are for you!

God, I love my neighbors. A text comes in from my family chat.

Winston: Good luck!

Mom: You'll do great!

Dad: Go get 'em, kiddo!

With a smile on my face, I walk into the hallway and glance toward Fletcher's bedroom. The door is cracked open. I heard him come out earlier to grab breakfast from the tray of goodies that were brought to our suite.

I'm about to call out that I'm heading down to get set up for the day when suddenly movement draws my attention closer to the open door. And then...abs. Holy shit! So many abs. What the hell does this man do at the gym? He looks like the business version of Kasen. I mean, I've seen photos of him online, but in the flesh, he looks even better.

A memory pops into my brain as my jaw falls open.

"If the men in our building were Ken dolls, what would their Ken doll name be?" Drew asks as he sips his margarita while lounging on our sofa.

I laugh. "You are ridiculous. You know that?"

He rolls his eyes dramatically. "Play along. Don't piss off the Queen."

I laugh again and set my martini down on the side table next to my favorite reading chair. "OK. Well, Bray is obviously Doctor Ken. And Kasen is, of course, Soldier Ken," *I start.*

"No way. Kasen is Spy Ken or like Undercover Ops Ken," *Drew declares and I snort with laughter.*

"OK. Gray is Composer Ken," *I say and Drew nods.*

"Oh, and with his body, Hutch is Viking Ken," *he states.*

"But he's not a Viking," *I protest, getting into this game more than I should.*

"Fine, he can be Football Ken," *Drew says with a sigh.*

I nod. "Al is Grandpa Ken."

We both nod in agreement.

"Troy is Dad Ken," *he adds.*

"What about me?" *he asks as he swirls his drink and then finds the part of the glass lip that still has salt and licks it.*

I give him a pointed look and he laughs. "I am not Gay Ken."

"Why not? And I wasn't even thinking that. I mean, not really," *I tease with a sheepish grin. I'd otherwise never tease any of my other friends like this, but Drew and I have been through so much together and I know talking about that topic is tough for him, even now.*

He glares at me.

"I love you," *I tell him because even if we joke with each other, I need him to know that I will always have his back.*

"I know," *he says like a petulant child.*

"How about...hear me out...Fashion Ken?" *I suggest.*

He purses his lips and furrows his brows. "Doesn't that already, like, exist?"

I shrug. "Who cares?"

"I care. I want a unique Ken name," *he protests.*

"Fine, you can be Diva Ken," *I say as I narrow my eyes.*

He cocks his head to one side and laughs. "OK, I can live with that."

We both laugh and then sit smiling at each other. "Now, what Barbie am I?"

My mind whips back to reality. I live in a world of Ken

dolls. How are all the men in my life so fit? What the hell? I never gave that a lot of thought, but now as I watch Fletcher pull a shirt over his head, I'm left drooling and contemplating all the abs in my life.

"Business Ken," I whisper.

His gaze abruptly shifts to the crack in the door and we stare at each other as he finishes pulling his shirt over his head. I'm not sure what he's thinking but a part of me that is in desperate need of sex is most definitely thinking about licking those abs and other things.

I've been caught red-handed, ogling my business partner. Partner? Yeah, I guess I'll go with that for now.

"You ready?" I ask, finally breaking the silence and hoping my face isn't as red as I think it might be.

"Yes. Let's go," he replies while his lips twitch and I know he's trying not to smirk. That smug bastard knows he's good-looking.

I spin on my heels and head out the door, a small part of me wishing that damn saltshaker was in my pocket. But instead, I have its twin and that will have to do for today.

As we approach the tent, cameramen are moving equipment. I trip on a wire and I feel Fletcher's hand on my hip, holding me steady. Once I'm upright and stable, he moves his hand to the small of my back, guiding me through the chaos to our station. It's a small thing. It's a gentlemanly thing. But it feels more than that.

When we reach our station, I shake the weird feeling I have. There's nothing between us. We've been thrust into a situation where we have to work together, and when it's over, we'll part ways and go back to being rivals. All will be right with the world.

Only, when I think about that future, it doesn't seem right. Can I hate Fletcher again? It feels wrong.

Fletcher grabs my apron from the hook where I left it and

hands it to me before grabbing the second one. We all have aprons with the show's logo on them.

And then, just like that, we start prepping. The filming starts mid-morning, and every time I feel like I've done something wrong, Fletcher is right there, encouraging me. We get the cookies in the oven and start cleaning up our workstation. It's unnerving doing it with a camera in your face.

My face falls and I go still when I realize I didn't set the timer. Shit!

I quickly go to the oven and turn the light on, peering inside. I can't tell.

"What's wrong?" Fletcher whispers in my ear, his strong body pressed to my back.

"I forgot to set the timer," I admit. I feel tears threaten.

His hand wraps around my upper arm and his thumb gives it the smallest rub. "It's alright. I set a timer on my watch as a backup. We have three minutes to go."

I immediately feel my shoulders relax.

I turn to face him. "I owe you...something," I manage.

He smirks and I roll my eyes. "Seriously? Do men not think of anything else?" I hiss, keeping my voice low in the off chance a boom with a microphone is nearby. Thank God we don't have microphones attached to us at the moment.

He shrugs. "Sometimes."

I roll my eyes again but then meet his gaze. "Thank you," I whisper.

He smiles. "I'm trying to be a good assistant. Now, let's get the frosting station ready."

I nod. His timer goes off and I pull the cookies out to cool. They look...perfect. Thank God!

He knocks my hip with his. "We did good, right?"

I grin at him. "We did. These look great. Let's just hope they taste as good as they look."

I check the timer and set a fan in front of the cookies. We

don't have any time to spare. "Give them one more minute to cool and then we have to get frosting," I state as I double-check our frosting.

I nod when I touch them. "They're ready. Let's get going," I command as we start icing the cookies. I taught him my technique yesterday and he has picked it up quickly. Before I know it, all three dozen cookies are done. I place them in the fridge for two minutes to set the frosting a bit and then we arrange them on the platter.

Our hands keep bumping into each other's, and as I set the last one down next to his, I feel his finger run along mine with intent. I look up at him.

"Win or lose, we did good," he states.

"You think?" I ask as I glance at our plate of cookies. I placed some decorative touches on the plate and it does look nice.

"I know," he insists and then gives a small chuckle.

"What?" I ask.

"Who would have guessed we'd make such a great team?" he confesses and I giggle.

"Not me," I admit as we both laugh.

The judges come around and sample each plate after we give a brief presentation of our cookies. I can't read them at all and I feel my palms sweating at my sides.

Just as they go to announce the winner of the round and which team will go home this week, Fletcher's hand wraps around mine and squeezes. His palm is sweaty too and I squeeze it back. This is crazy. How am I going to survive being this close to him for two more weeks without my growing crush turning into something more? I need to keep my head on straight. Falling for my rival and mortal enemy is not an option.

CHAPTER EIGHTEEN

Fletcher

I text Al again. It's the end of week two of the competition. Our pie got us to the finale round, but barely. If the other team hadn't overbaked their pie by a few minutes, we'd be done for.

Me: Any updates on the saltshaker?

Al: Not yet. I have Troy and Drew scouring the apartment. Roxy and Carly have had Phyllis checking in the café. Kasen even recommended looking around to make sure Licorice didn't hide it somewhere.

I frown. Who the hell is Licorice? I've heard some of the other names from Al and Camryn, but not that one.

Me: Who?

Al: Kasen lives in the building.

Me: No. Licorice?

Al: Oh, that's Roxy and Gray's cat. She likes to hide things.

Me: Got it.

Another message comes in from my sibling chat.

Spencer: Any progress on figuring her branding out so we can update ours?

Dalton: Ticktock. (clock emoji)

I groan. I've barely had time to think let alone consider my next business move.

Me: Not yet.

With each day that passes, I'm finding it harder to think of Camryn as my rival. I'll be the first to admit that it's been shocking to see how well we work together. Hell, I don't even mind that she's bossing me around in our little kitchen.

We've formed a rhythm and spend each evening planning. A small and growing part of me wishes we weren't rivals. I'm not even sure if I'd consider her the enemy any longer. And that bothers me. I should hate her or at the very least not like her. It's easier to hate your rivals.

I look down at the flowers Hutch sent over today. I had them arranged in our shared living space in the suite. I don't scare easily but that guy unnerves me. Camryn tells me he's a gentle giant, but I'm not sure I believe her.

Camryn walks in and grins as she steps up next to me. "How?" she asks, gently running a finger along a flower petal.

"Hutch sent them over," I explain, motioning to a note.

She picks it up and her smile widens.

"You really love your neighbors, huh?" I ask, frowning because I barely know mine. I admit I'm jealous of the rela-tionships she has with them all. I can't even say I have friends any longer. And the ones I do have, I often question if they stay friends with me for the perks and nothing else. I love my brothers and they are my friends, but I secretly long for the type of bond she has with all of these people.

"I do," she says as she sets the note down and looks up at me. "It's Thursday."

"And?" I ask.

"Didn't you say you needed to check on your store when we had a free day? Today is a free day," she points out.

We have a quick briefing this morning to confirm some things for next week but then we have the rest of the day.

I pull out my phone and call our family's driver to come get us.

"He'll pick us up in an hour," I say after I hang up.

"Who?" she asks.

"My driver," I state. She eyes me suspiciously and I return the look.

"You just call a driver and someone appears an hour outside the city to get us?" she asks incredulously.

"Yep. Just like that," I say. It's been so long since I thought about it. I remember one friend in college commenting once, but I run in circles where having a driver is a norm.

She rolls her eyes and I fight a smirk. Damn, she's adorable when she's annoyed.

"Come on," I add as I place a hand on the small of her back, guiding her down to our meeting. I wait for her to fight me, but she complies without any more attitude. What the hell is happening between us? First me, now her. We're both bowing to the other and it's a strange feeling as if the dynamic between us has shifted. We're sympatico and it feels natural yet foreign.

———

Three hours later, I'm waiting for her outside her store. She walks out and looks disheveled.

"Everything OK?" I ask, reaching out to tuck a stray curl behind her ear.

She lets out a long breath. "Phyllis forgot I changed the ordering system and under-ordered some ingredients and over-ordered others. She was trying to help, but now I have to fix it all. I think I got it mostly squared away." She pauses as if she's unsure if she should have even said all that to me.

I raise my hands. "We're still on a truce. We're on the same team for now. No judgments."

She eyes me suspiciously and then sighs. "Fine. Anyhow, uh..." She trails off and looks down at her phone.

"Want a drink?" she asks.

"Oh, uh, yeah, sure," I stammer as I look around. There's a local pub about a block away and I assume that's where we're going, so I start in that direction.

She laughs. "No. Not Joe's. Follow me." She motions across the street and I follow her into Al's building. We walk up a ridiculous amount of steps and then out onto the rooftop.

I stop as I take it in. I've been up here but it's been years. And it wasn't like this. I look at the covered bar and seating area, a lounge area with a few chairs, a fire pit, a hot tub, and a greenhouse.

"Wow," I manage, my voice breathy from walking up all the steps.

"Yeah. It's impressive, right?"

I nod.

She pats my back. "You need to work out more."

I glare at her and she grins. Al sees me and waves me over. I recognize Hutch immediately. He eyes me like he can't decide if I'm a foe or a friend.

A few other men are sitting near him. One with a little girl on his lap. Four women sit talking at a table with two older women and a couple my parents' age.

"Everyone, this is Fletcher. He's helping me with the competition, so be nice," Camryn says.

I get a lot of interesting looks. Some of them clearly hate me already and others can't seem to make up their mind.

"What'll it be?" Al asks.

"Do you have whiskey?" I ask.

He nods and pours me two fingers. I accept the glass with a nod.

"Who are you?" the little girl asks.

"He's what we call a wanker, Ava," Drew says from the door. I turn to see him coming out from the stairs.

"Unca Bray, what's a wanker?" she asks the man whose lap she sits on. He tries not to laugh.

"A naughty word, Ava," he says.

"I think it's spot-on," a larger man next to him mutters into his beer as Drew walks over to us.

Camryn whacks both Drew and the man on the back of the heads.

"Hey," Drew says. "Watch the hair."

The other man just glares at her. She sticks her tongue out and accepts a martini from Al.

"This is Kasen," she says, swatting the man's head again. He looks like someone who kills people, so I decide to be extra nice.

"Nice to meet you," I say.

He looks me up and down. "Yeah," he mutters.

Charming.

Hutch turns to me. "No offense, but you are in enemy territory here. This whole crowd is on Team Cam."

I chuckle and hold up my hand in defense. "I'd expect nothing less from her friends. However, I too am now on Team Cam." I pause. "I mean...literally. I'm her assistant for the competition."

Everyone freezes and I feel heads turning to look at Camryn and me.

"Amber's mom needed surgery," she explains with a shrug. "So for now, Fletcher and I are...well, having a truce of sorts."

"Of sorts?" Kasen mumbles.

"Yes. So be nice. We have the day off, so we came by to

check on our businesses. I needed a drink and this is the best happy hour in town," she says.

"Unca Bray?" Ava asks loudly to the man she's sitting on.

"Yes, little nugget?"

"Uh, why do we all not like this guy again?" she whisper-yells and points to me.

"Because he's Miss Camryn's rival. Remember, we were all talking about it the other day?" She frowns, clearly not understanding the words. "He's the one who wants to open a café on our street."

Now she's really frowning. "Right. But...we have one." She points to Camryn.

He smiles. "Yes, we do." He turns to me. "See, even children know that your store isn't needed. Best of luck with that."

Ava looks up at me as if trying to figure something out. "Mr. Drew. I don't think he's Satan. He doesn't have horns and he's not scaring me."

I spit out my drink and Drew laughs. "Well, Ava, I think Satan here doesn't want to scare people, so he puts on this nice Fletcher suit."

I glare at him.

Ava slinks back against the man who I presume is named Bray.

"He's joking, nugget," Bray says.

"Don't worry, I'm not Satan. I promise," I tell her.

She eyes me suspiciously. "Are you sure?"

Camryn leans in. "Yeah, are you sure?"

"For the love of...yes, I'm sure," I mutter and everyone starts laughing. "Come on over, Satan. Let's hear all about how you're helping our Camryn win this competition," Hutch says as he pats an empty chair next to him. And just like that, I learn that Camryn's neighbors are quite nice. I get why she likes them so much. And as the evening turns to night and I introduce myself and chat with all of them, I realize just how jealous I am of her life. It's everything that mine isn't.

I find myself watching Camryn with her friends. They all seem more like family. The fire pit is going, keeping the cold air at bay. Everyone has blankets and hats. Camryn throws her head back and laughs at something Margie says. The firelight brings out the red in her hair. She looks like a painting, too perfect to be real.

"Tread lightly there," Kasen says quietly and I realize he's watching me as I watch Camryn.

"Huh?" I ask, feigning ignorance.

"You hurt our girl and I'll kill you and no one will find your body," he says and grins. The smile should be reassuring like he's joking, but I also think he might not be.

"I promise, I won't hurt her. We'll figure something out," I say.

He leans in. "I don't mean the store thing," he adds.

Fuck.

"Yeah, I see you watching her. I'll repeat. Do. Not. Hurt. Her," he says again and claps me on the back. "Well, I'm off. Come on, Piper. I need to feed the babies."

I frown. They left babies downstairs.

Everyone sees my face and starts laughing.

Camryn leans in. "Don't worry. His babies live in a fish tank."

It takes me a moment to understand. "Oh, fish. Right."

She pats my leg. "You need another drink." She holds up her other hand and Al makes me a drink. I could get used to this. I wait for her hand to leave my leg but she leaves it there for a second and I start to want it there. In fact, I need it there, and when she pulls it away, I miss her touch. Shit. I'm falling for Camryn Tanner.

CHAPTER NINETEEN

Cam

I feel like something has shifted. I don't know what or when or why, but two nights ago as we sat back here in our suite and laughed over the antics of my friends, I felt at home with Fletcher.

I fell asleep with my head on his shoulder, our feet propped up on an ottoman we dragged across the living space. And when I woke, I was in my bed. He must have brought me in here after I fell asleep.

I smile at that as I start to wake up, snuggling beneath my blankets for a final few moments of silence.

Then the reality of the day hits me. We're about to start the finale. I'm proud of us and nervous as hell. So much rides on us winning. I need this. Phyllis is keeping the store afloat while I'm gone, but sales are down and McDowell's isn't even set to open for a few more weeks.

I get out of bed and head into the bathroom. I get ready as fast as I can and then meet Fletcher in the hallway.

"Ready?" I ask.

He nods. He had the driver pick up some more appropriate clothing for him for this week and he looks...well, like he belongs on television. I, however, look like a deranged, crazy cat lady who just saw daylight for the first time in a month. My hair, as much as I have tried, is its usual mess of curls. My skin is pale because I have no time for the sun. And my outfit, while clean, is from a thrift store that I went to with Jocelyn a few weeks ago. It all pales in comparison to Fletcher's high-end clothing and perfectly styled hair. The guy doesn't even need hair and makeup.

"What?" he asks as if sensing my annoyance.

"Nothing, just...nerves," I white lie because I am nervous.

"No worries. We got this." He holds a hand up for a high five and I raise an eyebrow.

"What?" he asks, keeping his hand in the air.

"Are we ten?" I question, fighting a smirk.

He looks me up and down and then with a heated stare shakes his head. I watch him swallow hard. His perfect lips press together before he speaks. "No, you are most definitely not a child, Camryn."

I feel my skin flush under his intense gaze. Holy shit, is Fletcher flirting with me?

I lick my lips and clear my throat. "Let's go," I command, not wanting to think anymore about Fletcher and what those perfect lips could do to me.

He only nods and presses his hand to my back as we walk out and down to the competition area.

My nerves double as I step up to the counter. We perfected everything yesterday and the prep day went so well that they decided to move up the competition day to today after both teams agreed we were ready.

I tie my apron and set out everything as the camera crew

gets ready. I feel my hand shake a little as I set down a knife and Fletcher's hand covers mine. I look up at him.

"We got this, Hollywood. Just like yesterday. Your cupcakes are going to win this thing," he says, reaching out with his other hand to twirl a loose strand of hair around his finger. He gives it a little tug and smiles down at me.

Felicity comes over with a grim look on her face and Fletcher's hand falls away. "What's up?" he asks.

She looks at me. "Small hiccup. A pipe burst in your room, Camryn. I had my PA get your things and place them in Fletcher's room while the staff clean up, but the room may not be habitable until after you leave. I can get a cot for the living room. But all the other rooms are booked and the nearest hotel has the crew staying in it and apparently fans for a local college football team. I'm so sorry. I just wanted you to know so you aren't surprised when you go up there later. Fortunately, the clothes in the closet are dry, so that's good," she says giving me a look of pity.

I sigh. "Thanks, Felicity. A cot is fine."

"She can have my room. I'll take the cot," Fletcher says.

We both look at him. "You won't fit on a cot," I say with a laugh.

He narrows his eyes. "Don't question me, Tanner. We'll make it work."

"OK, phew. Good. Now, go win this competition," she whispers as she looks around. "Don't tell the other team, but I'm rooting for you."

"Thanks," I manage.

Felicity leaves us to finish prepping and Fletcher places his hand on my arm as I go to turn. I look back at him.

"It's an omen. Something good will happen now," he says as if he's some kind of psychic.

"I hope so," I say as the show's director yells out directions and we steady ourselves for the last competition.

I'm silent as the judges stand at our station tasting my candied cranberry cupcakes with orange frosting. I've told them my inspiration story. Fletcher has stood silent, watching me do my thing.

I honestly can't tell what they're thinking. They asked similar questions of our competitor team, and now, I have no idea.

The head judge who is some celebrity chef on television sets down the remainder of the cupcake and looks at us and then at his two fellow judges.

"We'll be right back. We need to compare notes," he says and they all step outside the area to talk.

I feel sweat dripping down my back. I've never been so nervous in my life.

"I think I might die from anxiety," Fletcher mutters.

I laugh nervously.

I'm about to say I feel the same when the judges walk back inside.

"That was fast," I mutter under my breath.

They stand in the front of the area and look at both teams.

"It was a tough decision. Team Benson's Bakery, your chocolate mint cupcakes were delightful. They really brought out the peppermint flavor that many of us nostalgically remember at the holidays. And, Team Cam's Café, your candied cranberry and orange-frosted cupcakes were the perfect combination of flavors so many of us remember at holiday meals. But one team's cupcake stood out for its unique blend of flavors and textures. And so I am happy to announce the winner of this year's City Bake-Off is...Team Cam's Café," the head judge says.

I try to process what he's saying but I think I'm in shock. I stand there with my mouth falling open, my eyes wide.

"We did it!" Fletcher says excitedly as he picks me up and hugs me, spinning us both in a circle.

I laugh and throw my head back as I realize I did it. I might just be able to keep my dream café.

Fletcher sets me down and we grin at each other like fools.

"Congratulations," the head judge says as all the judges walk over to see us.

The next half hour is filled with congratulations and celebratory drinks. My head is spinning by the time we finally get back to our suite.

We walk in and I immediately note the cot in the living room. Shit. I completely forgot about that.

"You can have my room," Fletcher insists.

"No, I...Fletcher, that cot is so small. It's fine. I don't care," I state. I'm still riding the high of the win and I honestly couldn't care less if I slept on the floor.

"I care," he says and I turn to look at him. That heat is in his eyes again, the one that makes it feel like he's going to eat me alive.

I shiver under the intensity of whatever is happening between us. I haven't wanted a man this bad in...well, forever.

"I..." I swallow because I don't know what to say.

He places a single finger over my lips and I freeze. He steps forward and then again, backing me into the wall beside his doorframe.

"Hollywood, I've been wanting to do this for days. I shouldn't. I should go in that room and shut the door and then leave after tomorrow and go right back to wanting to evaporate your business, but I can't stop myself any longer. Not anymore," he says, his lips dangerously close to mine. His eyes search mine for something, maybe approval, consent. Who knows?

I lick my lips and bite the bottom one before I finally speak. "Then, don't," I manage.

And that's all it takes. His lips are on mine, his hands grip my ass and pull me up the wall. I respond with a yelp that only lets his tongue plunder my mouth. Holy shit, this is happening.

I wrap my legs around his waist and my arms around his neck. He squeezes me hard against him, pressing us to the wall. His tongue moves against mine. He tastes of the orange frosting and the candied cranberries. I swear he ate as many as we put in the cupcakes.

I feel his erection digging into my belly and I grind my center against it. He groans into my mouth.

Just that little noise has me wanting to rip off all my clothes and then his. I need him in a way I've never needed a man before. I don't understand what's come over me. Maybe it's winning. Maybe it's everything we've been through in the last few weeks. Whatever the reason, I start pulling at his shirt.

"Fletch, I need you," I whisper against his lips.

He pauses and I feel him smile. "You called me Fletch."

"That's your name, isn't it?" I ask, my lips trailing along his five o'clock shadow.

"Well, *Cam*, it is my name. And I like hearing that version of it from you," he replies, his head dipping and his mouth leaving a wet trail on my neck. I shiver under his touch.

"The one-bed issue is resolved," he adds as he walks us into his room, his hands clutching my ass, pressing me against him. "We're both in here tonight."

"We're sharing your bed?" I tease as I nip at his jaw.

"Yes, but there won't be any sleeping," he murmurs as he lets me slide down his front.

"Good, 'cause I'm not tired," I reply with a smirk. He reaches down and yanks my shirt over my head. For a few seconds, we're a frenzy of removing clothing, pulling and tugging until we're both naked.

"I knew you'd be perfect," he says in his deep, gravelly voice as his eyes rove over my body.

I feel goose bumps dot my skin, my body coming to life from his intense gaze. I look over his flawless muscled torso and then my eyes land on his penis and...I freeze. Holy shit! I had no idea Fletcher McDowell was so well-endowed. I swallow because it's been a few months and the last guy I was with wasn't small but he also wasn't this big.

Fletch raises an eyebrow and a full smirk graces his lips. I glare at him and his smirk widens.

"Get your ass over here, Hollywood," he commands with a crook of his finger.

I swallow hard and step up to him so we are toe to toe.

He cups my face gently in his hands and suddenly my anxiety notches down. I close my eyes and lean into his right hand a little. His thumb brushes gently over my cheek, while the other one combs through my hair, pulling out my hair tie and letting my curly locks fall across my shoulders.

"I love your hair," he whispers as he leans in and rubs his face along the side of my head and then down to my cheek where he kisses me softly. It feels so unlike him, this gentle, tender man is the exact opposite of the one I expected. How did I gauge him so wrong?

I hesitantly reach out and grasp his dick in my hand, rubbing up and down, a motion that wins me another groan.

"Tanner, get on that bed, right now," he growls and I shiver once more. His voice when he's commanding me to do something is so hot.

"Have you ever considered narrating a romance book?" I ask. I step away from him and get on the bed, lying back and slowly spreading my legs. His gaze travels down my body, lingering over my breasts before taking in the intimate folds between my legs.

He keeps his eyes on my sex as he answers, "No, Tanner. I haven't. But I'll gladly narrate what I'm about to do to you."

He positions himself between my legs and I can feel his breath on my sensitive skin that's already wet with need. "First, I'm going to eat this pretty pussy until you're begging me to let you come. Then..." He pauses for effect.

"Then, what?" I whisper breathily.

"Then, I'm going to roll a condom on and slide into this..." He trails off again and slowly runs a finger between my folds and then inside me. I let out a breath I didn't know I was holding. "Hot, wet, tight perfection. And I'm going to fuck you until you forget that we ever hated each other."

He looks up at me as if waiting for me to agree to his plans. How could a woman say no to that? I mean, seriously, who would turn this down?

Deciding I need to accept his proposal for the sake of all women everywhere, I agree with a small nod of my head.

"I need to hear it," he murmurs, blowing on my sensitive bud that's two inches too far from his mouth.

"Yes, yes, I want that too," I beg as I grasp his hair in my hands and push his face toward me. He chuckles for a second, but then swipes his tongue along my wet flesh and I practically convulse just from that one touch.

He takes that as a sign that I want more and he's right, I do want more, so much more. His tongue and finger start working me, testing the movements I like, waiting for my breath to hitch and my body to shake with the need to release.

And just when I'm about to come, he pulls back.

"Fletcher! Don't make me hate you again," I scold in frustration.

He grabs a roll of condoms from a bag near the bed and puts one on before climbing back over me. "Don't worry, Tanner, if anything, I'm a man of my word. And right now, I need to fuck you until you are screaming my name loud enough for the entire crew to hear it," he growls as he pushes inside me until he's buried to the hilt. My breath leaves my body again as I adjust to his size.

"You alright, Cam?" he asks after a moment of letting me acclimate, his face an inch from mine.

I nod. "Yes," I whisper as I look up at him.

"Good, 'cause I'm going to make you come so hard, you're going to remember this night more than the win we just had," he announces as he begins to move inside me.

CHAPTER TWENTY

Fletch

I don't know if it's the tension release from the competition, the exhilaration from today's win, or the pent-up sexual frustration of being around this gorgeous woman day in and day out for several weeks and not being able to touch her, but I feel like I've died and gone to heaven.

I look down at where our bodies are joined and fuck it's hot as hell. My gaze moves back up her body and I lean back and grasp her ankles, bringing them up on my shoulder so I can slide deeper. I watch as another inch of my cock disappears into her body. Damn, this woman is hot as fuck.

Her eyes roll back in her head and I watch her face contort as I move faster inside her. She's close. I can feel her muscles pulsing around me.

I reach between us and run my finger around her clit. Her breath hitches and her body clamps down on me.

"Fletcher!" she cries out as she climaxes. The combination

of her tight pussy gripping me and the sound of my name on her lips pushes me over the edge and I come with a grunt, emptying myself into the condom, wishing I could feel her skin around me.

I don't move for a minute as I keep myself propped up on my elbows. We both breathe heavily. I run my nose along her cheek, feeling her soft skin against mine. She smells of cupcakes and I grin at that. I love that she smells like a bakery. Maybe that's why I literally want to eat her.

Her body is soft and languid underneath mine. She looks perfectly satiated.

"I needed that," she admits with a giggle.

I open my eyes and meet her gaze. "*You* needed that?"

She nods and blushes, which only makes me want to repeat this whole thing again. I always thought she was beautiful, but now, seeing her like this, vulnerable and freshly fucked, she's breathtaking. What I first viewed as arrogant and argumentative qualities, I now see as determined and confident qualities in her. She's strong and passionate about her work. Her passion is addictive. Baking has never been that interesting to me. I know the basic mechanics of it, but in the past few weeks, I've loved it. It's been fun and rewarding. She's helped me find interest in what my family has done for over a century. That's something I didn't think anyone could do.

I pull out and dispose of the condom and then lie on the bed next to her, propping myself on my side so I can watch her.

She turns to face me. "You are unexpected," she says.

I raise an eyebrow. "*I'm* unexpected?"

She nods again and laughs. "Yes. If you had told three-week-ago me I'd sleep with you after the competition, I would have laughed at you."

I fight a grin. "I know exactly what you mean."

Silently, I'm wondering how I'll tell Spencer and Dalton or if I'll tell them. Shit, they'd be so pissed, or maybe they would think I did it to get more dirt on Camryn. Either way, I have no idea what happens now.

As if reading my mind, she asks, "So, what now?"

I lean over her and press my lips to her cheek, and then her jaw, and finally her swollen lips. I envision those lips wrapped around my cock and I feel all my blood draining to that appendage.

"Now," I say with a kiss. "We do that again."

She giggles as I place little kisses down her neck and then pay homage to both her breasts.

"I'm naming these," I say as I kiss one breast and then the other.

"What?" she says with a breathy laugh.

"Helga," I say as I kiss the right breast.

"And Heidi," I add with a kiss to the left breast.

"You can't name my breasts," she says laughing.

"Oh, I can and I just did," I state, licking around her right nipple and making her moan.

"Fine," she murmurs. "I get to name your penis."

My head pops up and I smirk.

"You already did that, didn't you?" she says. She rolls her eyes. "My friend Kylie once told me all about her brothers naming their dicks and I didn't think that was a thing, but Drew also swore it was."

I chuckle. "It is," I assure her.

She laughs again. "So, are you going to tell me his name?" she asks, glancing down at my erect cock that's ready for round two.

"I think you should guess," I say as I grab another condom and rip the foil packet open. I go to roll it down, but she presses a hand to my chest and pushes me back. She gets on her knees, takes the condom in one hand, and grips me in her other.

I swallow hard at the feeling of her soft hand wrapped around me.

"Carl?" she guesses. I laugh and shake my head. "Fred?" she says. I give her a pointed look. She shrugs. "Titan?"

"You're getting closer," I say.

She leans forward and presses a light kiss to the tip of my dick before taking me in her mouth and then her throat. Holy fuck! Camryn Tanner just exceeded all expectations.

I watch those swollen lips I just fantasized about as my penis moves in and out of her mouth. I breathe harder and I know I'm going to blow if she doesn't let up.

I pull myself from her mouth and she smirks with satisfaction as she rolls the condom down my length and crawls onto my lap.

With one hand holding my dick, she lowers herself onto me, inch by inch. We both let out a breath as she starts to move.

"Harry," she says.

"Huh?" I ask, forgetting our little game already.

"Mario?" she guesses again and I know she won't stop until she finds the name. Part of me wants to tell her, but this is too much fun.

"Nope," I reply.

She moves faster, clearly seeking her release. I grip her hips and slow her down, wanting to take my time and savor each second of sliding inside her wet, hot body.

"I'm going to guess, eventually," she says.

I lean forward and kiss her, moving my hands to cup her face as she moves on me. Our kiss gets sloppy, our tongues sliding in and out of each other's mouths. My hands roam to

Helga and Heidi and I caress them, flicking my thumb over her nipples, feeling them pebble under my touch.

When I pull back, we stare at each other and we stay like that as I reach between us, using my finger to push her over the edge. We come together as if our bodies were made to do this with the other. I've never felt this level of connection with someone while fucking them.

I'm not sure how I feel about it. I don't even want to contemplate it. Not now, maybe not ever.

Camryn gets off me and I toss the condom away. I crawl up the bed and pat the area beside me. She lies down, her head on my shoulder, her arm on my chest.

"Maybe we should switch places," I suggest.

"Why's that?" she asks, picking her head up and looking into my eyes.

"So I can sleep on Helga and Heidi," I state with a grin.

She rolls her eyes. "I can't believe you named them."

I waggle my eyebrows and she giggles, pushing at my chest before settling back down. I pull her closer and she wraps one leg over mine. I put my other hand on her thigh, rubbing it slightly. Her skin is so soft everywhere. I love that she has freckles. I want to spend hours memorizing each of them. A million things I want to do to her rush through my mind. I'm like a kid in a candy store.

"I need to go to the bathroom," she says, breaking my thought, although her voice tells me she wishes she didn't have to go. I let her up and she leaves.

"Zeus?" she yells from the bathroom.

I chuckle. "Nope."

She flushes the toilet and is back a moment later. She crawls back into my open arms and snuggles against me, settling back down with a leg over mine. I squeeze her to me, enjoying the feeling of her warm body and how it fits perfectly against mine.

"Arthur?" she whispers, her eyelids growing heavy.

"Go to sleep, Tanner," I command as I press a kiss to the crown of her head. She sighs and her breathing slows. I lie there for a long while, just listening to her soft breaths and wondering where we go from here.

CHAPTER TWENTY-ONE

Cam

"Well, that was horrendous," I state as we finish with the long media day. We're finally done with filming. We have a few media obligations when the show airs in a few weeks, but other than that, the competition is officially over.

"It wasn't that bad," Fletcher says as we pack up our things.

Apparently, because of my room situation, Felicity has gotten the filming company to comp me a weekend at another property. I don't have time to use it now, but I promised her I'd let her know when I had a free weekend.

Against my better judgment, I let Fletcher call his car service. I'm still trying to wrap my head around everything that's happened over the past two days.

My phone pings with an incoming text and I look down.

Drew: Celebratory happy hour tonight. Bring the enemy if you like.

I roll my eyes. I haven't told anyone yet that Fletcher and

I slept together. I don't even know where to start with that or how I feel.

I'm considering what to text Drew and then I realize I haven't heard from Max in a few days. Normally we text daily.

I'm about to text him before responding to Drew when Fletcher comes up behind me and buries his face in my hair. "I know what I want to do later," he says, pressing his growing erection into my back.

"Too bad. We have plans," I state as I hold up my phone, showing him the text from Drew.

He groans. "Can we rain check?"

I shake my head. "Nope. They will not let it go…" I trail off and turn around to face him. "What…are we doing, by the way?" I ask the obvious question because we haven't discussed what has happened between us.

He steps forward and cups my face. "I have absolutely no idea. But if you don't want to tell anyone yet, I'm alright with that."

I purse my lips as I consider what he's saying. "Let's keep it to ourselves for a little while. At least while we figure out what we're doing."

"OK, we'll keep it between you, me, Helga, and Heidi," he says. I roll my eyes and give him a little shove and he chuckles.

"Come on, the car is waiting," he says and we head out of the estate. It seems odd re-entering the normal world.

I'm quiet as the driver takes us back to my apartment building. Fletcher reaches over and grasps my hand, placing it in his lap, his thumb stroking my palm. I look down at our joined hands and wonder what upside-down world I've fallen into. I feel like Alice and I just went down the rabbit hole. Nothing makes sense.

I should hate Fletcher McDowell. I should be focused on using my winnings to ensure my business outperforms his. I should text Max and ask his advice, but right now, I just want to hang out with the people I care about, and if I'm honest, Fletcher is one of them.

The car stops outside my building and Fletcher helps me with my bag. We walk up to my apartment and drop it off before going up to the rooftop. There's a light snow tonight. Al has the heat lamps going and the fire pit.

Everyone turns when we open the door and yells, "Congratulations."

They have a cake and champagne. I get hugged by all my friends. They even shake Fletcher's hand, well, everyone except Margie and Cornelia who give him big hugs. He clearly won them over at the last happy hour with his discussion of Frank Sinatra songs.

"Pizza's hear," Hutch says as he walks onto the roof with a stack of our favorite pizza from the place down the street.

Everyone digs in. I grab two slices, realizing I haven't eaten since this morning. I'm famished and exhausted. But excited to be home.

"Are you famous now?" Ava asks as she sits on Bray's lap and eats a slice of cheese pizza.

"No. Not famous," I assure her.

"Oh. Well, maybe you'll be famous soon," she says with a big grin that's covered in pizza sauce.

Carly hands her a napkin and she rubs her face, smearing it more than wiping it away. Bray takes the napkin and wipes her face and she giggles.

"Unca Bray!" she yelps.

I'm two glasses of champagne into the evening and feeling great. I turn to Fletcher and decide now is the perfect time to mess with him.

"Frank," I state as I look at him.

He smirks and shakes his head.

"George?" I ask.

"Nope," he says as he takes a large bite of pepperoni pizza.

"Who's George?" Ava asks.

"No one. I'm just trying to...guess the name of Fletcher's very short, skinny friend with giant dark bushy hair," I say, my lips twitching.

Fletcher glares at me. "Hey, my friend is not short and skinny, and just so you know, he doesn't wear his hair long."

"What am I missing?" Drew asks, looking between us.

"Oh, nothing. Just a funny little inside joke," I state. I look back over at Fletcher and wink. He gives me a pointed look.

"Charles?" I mouth.

A smile ghosts his lips and he shakes his head.

"Is your friend's name Peter?" Ava asks.

Fletcher nearly chokes on his drink and I pat his back.

"Nope," he manages after a beat. I notice his cheeks are pink and I press my lips together to keep from laughing.

"Well, I think Peter would be the perfect name," I say giving Ava a big smile. She grins back at me.

"Me too," she says happily oblivious.

"Anyhow, thanks for throwing us a party," Fletcher says to Al.

Al nods and looks between us. "So, are we allowed to tell anyone that you won?"

I shake my head. "I cannot confirm nor deny that we won."

Everyone laughs.

"But it was a great experience," I say. I can see Roxy and Jocelyn give me suspicious looks and I know they are going to ask a ton of questions later. I'll need to come up with some explanation of why Fletcher and I are still being civil with one another.

Damn, this just got complicated.

"Did you talk to your family yet?" Al asks.

I shake my head. "Not yet. Winston is traveling for work and my parents are about to head out on a cruise. We've texted but I haven't spoken to them."

And I haven't texted Max yet, I remind myself.

"So now what?" Hutch asks as he looks between the two of us.

I furrow my brows in pretend confusion but I know exactly what he means. Will our truce continue? Are we back to being mortal enemies?

I have no idea how to answer that. *Oh, yeah, I'm fucking my rival now, so it's all good.* Nope. *Fletcher's dick is so good, I've forgotten all about that little competition between our stores.* Yeah, no.

"We actually found that we work well together and have a lot in common. So, for now, we're going to try to stay friends, right?" Fletcher answers him and I give him a grateful smile.

"Right," I agree.

Drew gives me a look that says we will most definitely be having a roommate conversation later tonight. I suddenly wish Fletcher and I could have remained in our little estate bubble for a few more days.

"We have some more media to do over the next week," Fletcher says. I glance over at him in confusion. We do not have any media. I have no idea what he's talking about.

"Right," I say, downing the rest of my drink.

"The show has us booked tomorrow night downtown, remember?" he says.

"Oh, uh, yeah," I play along.

"I thought you had no more media for, like, two or three more weeks?" Drew asks. Fuck, why do I have to tell my bestie everything?

"That's what we thought, but Felicity apparently added some additional interviews," Fletcher lies as he glances over at me.

"OK, I need to hit the hay," I state as I toss my paper plate away and set my champagne flute on the bar. We all take turns cleaning the dishes. "Shall I wash them?" I ask Al.

He waves me off. "Nope. The party is for you, we'll take care of it," he assures me. I hug him.

"Glad to have you back, kiddo," he whispers in my ear. And I squeeze him a little harder.

"It's nice to be home," I reply. While I love my family, there's just something about my apartment family. I'm not sure I'll live here forever, but I do know I will always be friends with them all.

I look over at Fletcher. He's standing and tossing his plate away too.

"I'll walk you out," I say, hoping for some privacy.

He nods, and with some goodbyes and hugs, we walk downstairs. His car is already waiting. "So more press, huh?" I ask.

He winks. "I needed a way to get you all to myself, Hollywood," he confesses.

"Nicely played, McDowell," I reply.

He looks around and then pulls me against him and kisses me, and not just some little peck. A full, open-mouth, tongue-against-tongue kiss that leaves me weak in my knees and wishing this pretend press event was tonight.

He pulls back and cups my jaw. "I'll see you tomorrow night."

I nod.

"Behave tonight. No spiders," he says.

I glare at him. "Not funny."

He smirks. "It's a little funny."

I roll my eyes as I fight a grin. I love hating this man. Maybe a little too much.

I walk back up to my apartment and immediately flop down on my bed. It feels good to be home.

"So are we going to talk about the fact that you are totally fucking Mr. Satan Reincarnated?" Drew says as he leans on my doorjamb.

I prop myself up on my elbows and look at my friend, the one man I tell everything to.

I smirk. "Nope," I say as I flop back down and stare at my ceiling. "We are not going to talk about that."

Drew comes into my room and lies down next to me.

"So we won't be talking about how he gave you *I want to fuck you right now* eyes all night? Or how he kept touching you or how when you weren't paying attention he was watching you?" he adds, turning his head to look at me.

"Yeah, we're not going to talk about any of that," I say.

"A shame, I could use some good raunchy details of a torrid love affair with one's mortal enemy. I guess I'll just have to go steal a book from Roxy's bookstore," he says with a sigh.

"I don't think it's stealing when you buy them," I say with a laugh.

"True. But back to you. Please tell me he was a god in the bedroom," he pleads.

I giggle and pretend to zip my mouth closed.

Drew turns on his side and looks at me. "Like *you're sore* big or *you won't be walking for days* big?"

I turn on my side. "Like *I'm ruined for all men from here out* big," I answer.

"Damn," he says and rolls onto his back. "Too bad we won't be talking about that hypothetical life-altering sex you had."

I roll onto my back again and lean my head against his shoulder. "Yeah, it really is too bad. Because I'm pretty sure his tongue was made to please."

"Damn, this hypothetical is hot," Drew murmurs.

"It really was," I reply.

"Was?" he asks.

"Is, was, I don't know," I admit.

"Sounds like you have some thinking to do," Drew says as he sits up and pats my leg. "I'll leave you to it. I need a cold shower after all this hypothetical sex talk."

I giggle. "You're sick."

"Takes one to know one," he says and air-kisses me before leaving me alone with my thoughts. But I only have one thought...could this thing between Fletcher and me actually work?

CHAPTER TWENTY-TWO

Fletch

I float on a raft in my parents' indoor pool. It's been twenty-four hours since I dropped off Cam. I miss her. I miss her sassiness, her stubbornness, and her sexiness.

"You trying to drown yourself in here?" Spencer's voice rings out from the far side of the pool.

I look over and see he's about to dive in and I close my eyes. While we were all on the swim team as kids, none of us ever dive properly into the pool. It's always a cannonball.

A splash covers me in water droplets.

"Asshole," I mutter.

"What's crawled up your ass?" he asks as he swims over to me and treads water.

"Just thinking," I confess as I use my hands to push me farther from him.

"Don't think too hard, Fletchy," Spencer teases, using my childhood nickname.

"Don't be such a prick, Pencer," I tease back, using the

nickname that came from him not being able to pronounce his own name.

He flicks me off and starts swimming laps. I have no idea how to tell him and Dalton that I slept with Cam. I don't even know what I'm doing. Do I continue opening the store? Do I sabotage it so I don't kill her dream? I'm so fucking confused.

"Seriously, what is eating at you?" Spencer says after finishing a few laps.

I sigh and sit up. It's time to rip off this bandage. I can't lie to my brothers. They'll know.

"I slept with Camryn Tanner," I admit.

He freezes, his face contorting in confusion. "Like, to get more intel?"

I shake my head. "She's not like how I thought she would be. She's...smart and savvy, and I like her, Spence," I confess.

"Shit, bro. That is bad news. She's going to hate you when we put her out of business," Spencer says.

"I'm done trying. I'm just going to give it my all with our store, and if it fails, then it fails," I say.

"No way. You can't fail. Dad will have a shit fit. What the fuck, Fletcher? You know we need this store to succeed," he says and I can see him starting to get angry, which Spencer doesn't do often, but when he does, it's epic.

I put my hands up trying to placate him. "Listen, I have some ideas. I think we can both be successful. We can... complement each other," I offer. Do I have ideas? Sort of. Will they be successful? Maybe.

But I'm not letting Spencer be the reason things don't work out between Cam and me. I really do want to give this a proper try.

"Good luck introducing your new flavor of the month to Dad," he says and pauses. "You know what, never mind, make sure I'm there and have popcorn."

He swims to the edge and pulls himself up. "I can't believe you'd let your dick get in the way of our company. That's low even for you, Fletch."

He shakes his head and walks away before I can argue with him. I splash the water angrily and get out. I hate that my entire family holds my misspent youth over my head. I'm not that boy anymore. It's been well over six years since I acted anything but a gentleman from a well-respected family.

And I would certainly not sleep with someone just to spy on them. What the hell is Spencer even going on about?

I need to talk to someone who doesn't view me like my family. I just don't know who...or do I? I decide to text a friend online and seek some advice. Too bad I can't just ask my own fucking family members.

One hundred dollars says Spencer has already called Dalton.

As if on cue, my phone rings and I see Dalton's name flash across the screen. Great.

"Yeah." I pick up as I dry myself with a towel.

"You fucking slept with her!" Dalton yells.

"Calm down before you give yourself a coronary," I insist with a roll of my eyes.

"You cannot be fucking serious?" he screams. Great. Pissed-off Dalton is a million times worse than angry Spencer. Spencer will calm down by tomorrow but Dalton will hold a grudge for the next ten years.

"I like her," I seethe through gritted teeth.

"You like her? *You* like her! Well, great, let's just all sing kumbaya and call it a night," he says, his voice laced with sarcasm.

I run a hand through my wet hair. "You don't understand. I was wrong about her. She's not who I thought she was. You'd like her if you gave her a chance," I try to explain.

"You think I go hanging out with everyone who runs

competing businesses? No. Because I don't want them to know our company's secrets. How will you even be able to trust her?" Dalton asks.

He raises a good question. Shit. I wish we had had more time to figure things out before people knew we were together or whatever the hell we are.

"I got to go," I say.

"We'll talk about this later," Dalton assures me and I groan as I disconnect. Right now, I need to calm down and the only thing that will relax me is seeing a certain spunky redhead.

————

I watch her close up her café and I smile as she dances around with a mop. I'm sitting on a bench that looks recently placed outside the bookstore. I'm so intrigued by the beautiful woman across the street that I don't notice Al.

"Am I interrupting you?" Al asks.

I jump a little. "Shit, you scared me," I say as I try to calm my racing heart. I know my cheeks must be pink from being caught ogling his neighbor. Thankfully, it's dark out.

"Sorry about that. Just going for my nightly stroll," he says as he sits down next to me.

"Hey, Al. Hi, Fletcher," Hutch calls out from the entrance to the park at the end of the block.

"Hi," I say, confused why he's dressed in camo and walking around the city at night.

"Anything?" Al asks.

Hutch shakes his head. "Nope. Just Troy going for an evening walk. Oh, and Joe. I'm shocked he took the night off from the tavern. And Bray went for a run before work."

"Well, best you get inside. Looks like we might get some snow tonight," Al says to him.

Hutch looks up at the sky. Clouds are starting to roll in, blocking the moonlight.

"Good. Snow will mean tracks and that means more clues," Hutch says with a grin as he walks inside.

"He's obsessed with those flowers, huh?" I ask, remembering the first day I met Hutch.

"Something like that," Al agrees.

We're quiet for a few minutes as we both watch Cam. She's shaking her ass now while wiping down counters. Adriana comes into view and the two of them duet to whatever song they are listening to.

"Cam's captured your heart, huh?" Al finally says, breaking the silence with words I'm not ready to hear.

"I'm sorry, what?" I ask, feigning ignorance.

He uses a cane to point to Cam. "That one is special. I've seen her grow into a strong woman. She needs an equally strong man. Are you up for that challenge?" he asks.

I fight a smirk. Fucking Al O'Brien. The man is a classic romantic. I remember seeing him with his late wife, and even as a kid I knew that they were how love should be.

"She's different than I thought she'd be," I admit.

"Well, she's guarded. She doesn't show her true colors to just anyone. You must have gained her trust somehow," he explains.

"How can it even work though? I feel like we're Romeo and Juliet. We're destined for disaster," I confess because I need to talk to someone and Al seems like Switzerland compared to my brothers.

He smiles. "Love has a sneaky way of working out, if you just try. You'll figure it out. I have faith in you. Maybe your business needs a little tweak. You're a smart man, Fletcher McDowell. I see a lot of your grandfather in you. Don't listen to those troublemaker brothers of yours. Follow your heart and you'll always win." He pauses and stands up. "Well, off to stretch the old legs. You have a good night."

He tips his hat and walks toward the lit path in the park. I want to tell him to be careful but I have a feeling Al does this every night. Hell, he probably knows every inch of this neighborhood better than anyone.

Adriana leaves and Cam turns the lights off before locking the front door. She falters slightly as she turns to cross the street and sees me sitting on the bench.

"Hey," she says softly as she approaches me.

"Busy?" I ask.

She shakes her head. "Why?"

I shrug. "Just thought I'd see if you wanted to hang out. Maybe watch a movie," I suggest.

"Oh, well, Drew is watching a reality show," she says, motioning to her apartment above us.

"We can go to my place. I have a movie room," I offer.

She smirks. "Shocking," she says in a mocking tone and I laugh.

"I know, right," I tease.

"Fine. Just let me grab some things and change," she says as she lets me into the building. "What should we watch?"

"*Arachnophobia*?" I state.

She punches my arm and I smirk. Yeah, coming here was the right thing to do. Screw my brothers, Al is right. Cam is worth fighting for.

CHAPTER TWENTY-THREE

Cam

Fletcher inspects every square inch of my apartment as he waits.

"Who's this?" he asks, pointing to a photo of me with my grandmother, the one whose saltshaker is missing.

"That's Gan-gan," I reply while I stuff some toiletries into my overnight bag. I used to be better prepared for the new relationship getting-to-know-you conversations. I used to sleep with men, but lately, it's all been about the café.

"And this?" he asks, pointing to a family photo.

"Those are my parents, my brother, Winston, and me," I state, grabbing clean underwear while he's not looking.

"And—"

I cut him off. "That's me and Drew on spring break. That's our friend Kylie. That's her brother, he plays base-ball. And that's Drew, me, and Drew's cousin. And that's all of us on the rooftop. And that's me, Carly, and Ava at the zoo last year. And that's a photo of me with my cousins at a family reunion a few years ago," I rattle off because I'm tired of the back and forth. I'm generally just tired. It was a long day. I'm still sorting out everything that went awry while I was away. Phyllis did all she could but things happened, orders were placed incorrectly, and invoices needed to be paid. It'll take me at least two weeks to sort all of this out.

I turn back to my bag and toss in some other clothes. "OK, I'm ready," I say as I spin around to face him.

He's stepped up behind me so we're chest to chest or stomach to chest. I look up at him and he cups my jaw. "You have a lot of people in your life," he says and his voice has a hint of sadness. Does he not? I realize how little I know about him. I obviously know who his family is. But aside from a few lighthearted stories he shared about his brothers and the superficial information on the internet, I really don't know much about him.

I give him a small smile. "I guess I do. Although, some of them are annoying," I say, trying to lighten the mood. I gesture toward the living room where Drew is watching the latest episode of some reality television series about people falling in love on an island.

I zip up my bag and he grabs it, pausing at the photo of me and my grandmother. "The missing saltshaker was hers?" he asks, motioning to the photo.

"Yeah. She taught me how to bake," I say, remembering all the times I helped her in the kitchen. She always seemed to be in the kitchen, cooking or baking something or maybe those are just my favorite memories of her.

"You look a little like her," he says as he examines the picture.

"A little," I agree, walking out to the living room. He follows me and Drew looks up from where he's snuggled up on the sofa.

"I'm going to watch a movie over at Fletcher's place," I say.

He eyes me and then the overnight bag Fletcher is carrying. He smirks. I glare.

"Have fun *watching* the movie," he says, giving me an overly sweet grin.

I sort of want to hit him over the head, but I refrain.

I see him look over at Fletcher and he nods. Frowning, I glance back at Fletcher who is looking at me. What the hell was that about? I'm about to ask when there's a knock at the door.

"Asswipe, you coming down for game night?" Kasen yells.

"Oh, shit. I forgot about that," Drew says as he runs toward his room. I roll my eyes and open the door to find my large, ex-military neighbor standing there.

"Where's Drew?" he asks, stepping into the apartment.

"Please, come in, Kase," I mutter.

"I will," he agrees and then stops and looks at Fletcher.

"Where are you going?" he asks us, looking Fletcher up and down.

"Just to watch a movie," I say, wanting to get away from Kasen because I feel like he knows more than he's letting on. I wonder if he found anything when he was looking up stuff about Fletcher and the new store. He hasn't said he's found anything yet but the way he's staring at Fletcher is making me uneasy.

"OK, gotta go," I say and quickly pull Fletcher into the hall and down the stairs.

"Slow down," he says with a laugh.

We get out onto the street and I catch my breath.

"Cam, what the hell?" he asks, now looking concerned as I lean over and breathe. Damn steps! I wish Al would put in a new elevator. I know we'd all have to chip in to pay for it, but right now, I would love to have that.

I hold up a finger. After a few breaths, I stand back upright. "Just in a hurry to go watch a movie. And Drew would have talked our ears off."

"And here I was worried about Kasen," he mutters as he opens the car door for me.

I grimace. Should I tell Kasen to call off his attempt to find dirt on Fletcher? I mean, it was just an innocent ask for information, not anything super nefarious.

"Kasen's...intense," I manage as he shuts the door and then gets in next to me.

"Intense? He looks like someone who kills twelve people at a time with his bare hands," he says. I giggle. He gives me a deadpan look.

"Look, Kasen is like a...well-trained tiger? He's completely docile and you can rub his belly, but if you cross that line... yeah, he'd probably kill you," I admit.

"Rub his belly?" Fletcher looks at me with a raised eyebrow.

I blush. "You know what I mean," I huff as I look away and scan the people walking in the city. I do love it here. Growing up in the suburbs is nice but there's just something about the anonymity of walking around city streets. You're with people, but you can also be invisible at the same time.

I feel Fletcher's hand on my leg and I glance down. The memory of what that hand can do to my body has my lady bits coming to life. I feel my blush turn into a full-body flush.

"Are you hot?" Fletcher asks as he reaches down and adjusts a temperature dial.

"No. I-I'm fine," I stammer as I try to pull myself together. What are we doing? Am I making a huge mistake?

I look over and he's watching me intently. I'm about to say something when the car comes to a stop. I look up and see we are at a fancy high-rise downtown. I nearly roll my eyes because this is exactly the type of place a billionaire would live. Oh shit, he probably is a billionaire. Why I never thought about this until right now, I have no idea.

My level of feeling flustered just skyrocketed.

I'm about to open my door when I realize Fletcher is already there opening it. He extends his hand to me and I begrudgingly accept it. I hate all this gentlemanly shit, but I'm too far in my mind to care at the moment.

He does that thing where he places his hand on the small of my back, guiding me inside the building where he greets a doorman and then presses his thumb on a security panel beside the elevator. It opens and we enter. There are only four buttons and he presses one.

Huh?

The elevator takes off at a speed I realize would never work in my building because when I look closer, I see level 30. OK, then, that's a few levels higher than our building.

The door opens and we are in a foyer with double doors. Fresh flowers sit on a circular table with some sort of inlaid wood design.

He presses his thumb to a panel beside the doors and a lock sounds. He opens the door and I step inside and am greeted by the most amazing view of the city.

I walk toward the floor-to-ceiling window, ignoring the rest of the room. Gazing out, I see the water, the buildings, everything, all of it lit by lights. It's beautiful. I can only imagine what the sunrise looks like here.

Fletcher comes up behind me and wraps his arms around my waist, resting his chin on the top of my head.

"You like the view, Hollywood?" he says in his incredibly deep voice.

I shiver from his touch and he tightens his grip on me.

"It's beautiful," I manage. I turn in his arms and look up at him.

"What are we doing, Fletch?" I ask as he peers down at me.

He sighs. "I have zero ideas."

"We...how does this work?" I ask, trying to find the right words.

"Well, first, I take you to my bedroom and then..." He trails off and smirks and I groan, giving his chest a little shove.

"You know what I mean," I say with exasperation.

"I know, Camryn," he replies. He steps back and holds out his hand. It feels like a pivotal moment, if I don't take his hand, this all ends and we go back to hating each other, and if I do...well, I have no idea.

He's patient as he watches me consider what I'm going to do. I don't know why, but something my grandmother used to say pops into my head.

Grab life by the horns and enjoy the ride.

Should I throw caution to the wind? How can I ever truly trust him? If I pursue whatever this is and then it blows up in my face and ruins my business, will everyone in my life give me the *I told you so* look? Probably. Do I care at this moment? Not really.

Without a word, I place my hand in his and he tugs me against him, our lips colliding.

"Right decision, Tanner," he whispers as he kisses me. He pulls back a little and cups my face. "I promise, we'll figure it all out later. But right now, I want you in my bed."

I swallow hard. In his deep voice, that sounds super fucking hot.

"OK," I reply.

He grins like a kid who just won a board game. Only, I'm worried that we're playing chess and I might have just exposed my king.

But when his lips find mine again, I forget everything else...for now.

CHAPTER TWENTY-FOUR

Fletch

I hit the lights and push the dimmer, turning to survey Camryn. She's stopped in her tracks and is wide-eyed.

"What's wrong?" I ask.

"Y-your room," she says as she looks around us.

I turn and look at my room. It looks perfectly normal to me. Looking back, I watch as she steps further into the space. Her eyes follow the furniture around the perimeter of the room. It's sparse. My clothes are in my closet. My room has a large bed and nightstands. A small table by the entrance with a few drawers. And a sitting area in front of the slider door that opens onto a small balcony. There's a floor-to-ceiling mirror in a gold frame opposite the bed. And above the bed is a painting by an artist friend of mine. The coffered ceiling has a gold inlaid design that surrounds the painting. The walls of the room are a black-on-black design. The light wood floors running throughout my apartment continue into my room.

"It's...enormous," she whispers as she stands in the middle of the room and spins with her arms out.

I feel my lips twitch but I'm too desperate to be inside her right now to be distracted by her amusing antics.

I walk up behind her and wrap my arms around her waist. We stare at each other in our reflection in the mirror. I splay my hand possessively over her abdomen and for a flash of a second I imagine an entire life with her. Children, a home, vacations, a shared bakery, late-night laughing, and passionate sex.

I blink away the thought faster than it emerged from the recesses of my mind.

"What?" Cam asks, raising her face to peer up at me from beneath her lashes.

"Nothing," I lie as I lean down to kiss her, hoping it will make us both forget whatever it was I just did or thought.

She turns in my arms and I decide we need a distraction. I pull her top off over her head. She kicks off her shoes. I unbutton her jeans and push them and her underwear down her creamy thighs until they fall to the ground and I'm on bended knee. She undoes her bra and it falls next to us. She puts a hand on my shoulder as she pulls her foot from her socks, jeans, and underwear and then does it with the other foot, kicking the clothing to the side.

I look up at her. She watches me with a smirk and I return it while kissing her between her legs. Her skin pebbles telling me that no matter how calm, cool, and collected she pretends to be, she's not immune to my touch.

I continue to lick and suck the wet flesh until her hands grip my hair and her body trembles.

"Fletcher," she groans. I grin against her. She needs more.

I stand and she tugs at my buttons on my shirt. I assist and we slowly remove my clothing.

When we're both standing naked, I lift her and set her on

my bed. I decide I want a show tonight. Instead of crawling up the bed, I sit behind her and pull her back against my front. I hook her legs over mine and spread them wide.

We both stare at our reflection in the mirror in front of the bed.

I reach down separating her folds, running my finger up and down, and coating it in her wetness. My skin glistens with it as I skin two fingers into her. Her mouth falls open but her gaze stays locked on the erotic scene in front of us.

I lean my mouth to her ear. "Look how fucking perfect you are," I whisper as I start moving my fingers in and out of her heat.

It's like my personal wet dream. I've done things like this before, but somehow it feels different tonight.

She moans as I stretch her, so I can penetrate deeper. I begin to work her harder and faster until I feel her muscles clench around me and her eyes squeeze shut as she cries out my name. I watch her release coat my fingers. Slowly, I pull them free and bring them to my mouth to taste her again. Fuck, this is hot and I want so much more with her.

I flip her over and we stare at each other as I sink inside and then remember I need a damn condom. Shit.

I pull out and her brows furrow.

"What's wrong?" she asks, her legs wrapped around me.

"Condom," I say as I look down and see my wet dick.

Her eyes search mine. "We probably should, but…" Her voice trails off and I look down at her.

"What?" I ask.

"When were you last with someone?" she asks and I roll to the side, so I'm not on top of her.

"About three or four months ago," I admit. It was a hookup with a woman I used to see periodically when I was in London.

"And did you have any checkups since then?" she inquires.

"Yes. I had a full annual exam and bloodwork about a month ago," I answer still confused as to why we are discussing this.

She nods and presses her lips together. "It's been a long time for me. But I've had some health stuff that requires I take birth control," she says.

"Health stuff?" I ask.

She nods. "I get really bad cramps and some other issues surrounding my period. There's not a lot doctors could do for it, but taking the pill does help a bit, so I do it."

I pull her toward me. I hate that she has to deal with that.

"Can I trust you?" she whispers. "I really want to trust you, Fletcher," she adds, her eyes glaze a bit and I suddenly feel like such an ass. We should have been talking about so much more than just hooking up. There are a million unanswered questions between us. I don't have all the answers, but I know whatever is happening between us is important, more important than a store.

"Yes, Camryn. I won't let business come between us. We'll figure it out. I promise," I assure her.

"I want to believe you," she says and it's a sucker punch to my gut.

"You don't?" I ask.

She shrugs. "I sort of do, but it's hard. I...things between us changed so quickly, I'm still trying to get my bearings. I want to give us a real chance, but I also can't lose the café. It's my life. I've worked so hard for it," she confesses, her eyes welling.

A stray tear escapes and slides down her cheek. I lean in and lick the salty liquid away. "We are not going to let business come between us. I promise you that. You have my word," I assure her. But beneath my calm surface, I'm worried. Will my family accept her? Can I figure out a way for both our businesses to thrive?

"OK," she whispers. "We'll figure it out together," she adds with a small smile. Her legs wrap back around mine and I sink into her. I can't remember the last time I went without a condom, and never so soon in a relationship, but this feels different. This feels real as if every relationship before her was only practice.

We move in silence, our gazes locked. I move faster, chasing my release, needing to come inside her, to make her mine. It sounds ridiculous and I feel like an idiot thinking that, but some primal part of me wants to mark her in some small way.

"Don't stop," she whispers, her legs cross behind me, pulling me deeper inside her.

"Come, Cam, I need you to come, baby," I whisper as I feel my balls tighten.

Her eyes squeeze shut and I lean down and kiss her while her body's inner muscles convulse around me. And that's all it takes for me to lose control and follow her over the edge into an abyss of pure ecstasy.

We both pant, our foreheads touching.

"Are you going to give me a tour of your palace, or are you keeping me locked up in your bedroom?" she asks.

I laugh and run my nose along hers. "I'd like to keep you locked up in here, but I have a feeling you'd end up exploring this place on your own," I say as I begrudgingly pull out of her and roll us over so she's lying on me.

She settles herself between my legs and places her hands, one on top of the other, on my chest with her chin on them.

"My entire apartment would fit into your living room," she says.

"So?" I reply because I don't care about that.

"We come from different universes. How is this going to work exactly?" she asks.

"We will figure it out," I assure her.

"Will we?" she questions, her abdomen pressing into my softening dick, making it come back to life.

I tug on a strand of her red hair. "Stop being so stubborn. We can figure things out, but right now, I want to concentrate on more important things," I say and thrust my hips up against her.

"You are like a racing car. You have a recovery time of like two seconds," she laughs.

"I feel like we should test that theory a few more times," I say with a smirk and she laughs again.

I roll us back over and stare down at the woman who I am falling for in a matter of only a few weeks. "I'll give you the princess tour tomorrow morning. We have more important things to work on right now," I tease as I nip at her jaw.

"I suppose I can live with that compromise...for now," she murmurs as she leans her head back to grant me access to her neck.

"I love a good compromise," I reply, leaning in and running my tongue down the column of her neck. Maybe we can figure out a business compromise too? Maybe, just maybe, things can work out between us.

CHAPTER TWENTY-FIVE

Cam

I stretch my legs over his muscular calves. Smiling without opening my eyes, I burrow against Fletcher. He's warm and his right arm is wrapped possessively around me. It tightens as I move.

"Ten more minutes," he groans.

I giggle. "Five more minutes," I protest.

"Please tell me you aren't some annoying morning person," he murmurs.

"I'm a morning person and it's already..." I trail off and realize I have no idea what time it is.

"Gretchen, what time is it?" Fletcher says loudly.

Gretchen? Who the hell is Gretchen?

"The time is nine fifteen," an automated voice answers.

"You named it Gretchen?" I ask as I start to attempt to sit up, but he pulls me back against his chest.

"Yes. Do you have an issue with that?" he asks.

"Uh, no, I guess not," I answer as I contemplate this. "What else does she do?"

I refuse to have one of these at the apartment, but Bray has one and loves it. I think he renamed his something funny like Mrs. Doubtfire, from a film that Ava loves.

"Oh, you know, the normal stuff, thermostat, preheating the oven, changing the floor temperatures, starting the shower, turning on appliances, and stuff like that," he says as he yawns.

I raise my head. "Floor temperatures?"

"Yes. The floor is heated," he explains. "Are you hungry?"

I nod. "Famished."

"Gretchen, order a half dozen assorted bagels with regular cream cheese and two cappuccinos from Mo's Bagels on Fifth Street," he says.

"Ordering a half dozen assorted bagels with regular cream cheese and two cappuccinos from Mo's Bagels on Fifth Street," she repeats in her computer voice. "That total will be fifty-two seventy charged to the card on file. The order is estimated to be delivered in twenty-seven minutes."

He looks over at me. "I wonder what we could do for twenty-seven minutes?" he ponders with a smirk.

"My God, does your dick ever rest?" I ask, raising an eyebrow.

"Olympic gold medalists have to work constantly," he replies as he waggles his eyebrows and I giggle.

"You mean Trevor?" I tease.

"Not his name," he replies with a grin.

"Cesar?" I ask.

He shakes his head and rolls me beneath him. Then I hear a door opening.

"Flucker! Where are you?" a voice calls out.

"We were going to grab Mo's and then go to Mom and

Dad's house. Oh wait, they are coming over here," another voice says.

"Seriously? Why?" the first voice asks.

My eyes widen. Shit? Are these his brothers? Please be his brothers. Oh, wait, fuck, no, no brothers. Oh God, am I about to meet the other McDowell brothers? I was supposed to make a good first impression when I was going to sabotage their new store. And now, I actually do want to make a good first impression. Shit!

"Get dressed," Fletcher says as he gives me a quick kiss. "Coming!" he yells to his brothers.

I smirk and mouth, "You wish."

He glares at me and I make a sad face. And step toward his bathroom with my overnight bag.

He takes three strides and cages me against the wall. I look up at him and see the heat in his eyes.

"Oh, I will come, Tanner," he whispers against my lips. "And so will you."

"Promises, promises," I tease.

He presses his hand between my legs, sliding a single finger inside me, and groans as he feels how wet I am. "You want me to make you come like this?" he asks, his deep voicing practically making me convulse on the spot.

"What the fuck are you doing in there?" a voice calls out.

"Or who are you doing?" a second voice says with a chuckle.

I feel my cheeks heat as I keep my gaze on Fletcher.

His jaw tics as his brothers speak, but instead of leaving me, he adds a second finger. I feel my body begin to tense. I'm not sure if it's the thrill of nearly being caught or the intense way he's watching me come undone against his wall, but I'm hurdling toward my release.

As if he senses it, his fingers work me faster, his thumb

caressing me just where I need it, and I come hard. A silent cry escaping my lips as I ride the wave.

He kisses me gently and pulls his fingers from me, licking them clean in a seductive way that has me nearly coming again.

"Go get dressed," he whispers as he places a gentle kiss on my lips and smacks my ass.

I manage to stay standing when he steps away and I hurry to shower and put on my clothes. I silently curse myself for not bringing a nicer outfit. Am I ready to meet the other McDowell brothers?

I know the oldest is Dalton. He has a reputation of being cutthroat. Spencer is the middle brother. In photos, he looks like a hot, nerdy version of Fletcher.

But what will they think of me?

I tie my hair back and slick it with some water, hoping to keep my unruly curls from escaping, a near impossible task.

Walking out, I hear some hushed voices. I strain to listen but can't make out what they are saying. As I turn the corner into the living room, I can see Spencer standing in front of the windows, his hands in his pockets. Dalton and Fletcher seem to be in an argument.

Fletcher's eyes meet mine and Dalton turns to look at me.

"Hi," I squeak, sounding like a total idiot.

Spencer turns and surveys me like I'm a car he's considering purchasing. Dalton just gives me a look that says he trusts me about as much as I trust my two-year-old Wi-Fi router.

"This is Camryn Tanner," Fletcher introduces me and wraps a protective arm around my waist. I lean into his shoulder and his hand squeezes my hip in a reassuring manner.

"Nice to meet you both," I say nervously.

Dalton extends a hand and I shake it. Spencer gives me a nod from the window.

"So, you two are...dating?" Dalton asks.

"Yes," Fletcher says without missing a beat. His hand squeezing my hip again.

"And what about your businesses?" Spencer asks as he leans against the windows and crosses one leg in front of the other.

"We'll figure it out," Fletcher responds. I feel as if I'm in hostile territory. I'm about to excuse myself when there's a knock at the door. A moment later, Dalton opens it to allow Fletcher's parents to enter. I only know who they are because I've seen them online. Holy hell! If I didn't give off deer-in-headlights vibes before, I most certainly do now.

"Mom, Dad, this is Camryn Tanner, my girlfriend," Fletcher announces.

I feel the color drain from my face as I stand in front of a very well-dressed middle-aged couple.

"Oh? Girlfriend? Why didn't you tell us?" his mother says as she pulls me into a hug.

"I'm Christine and this is Eddie. It's so nice to meet you," she says as she pulls back. She smells amazing. Do all rich people smell good? What's up with that?

His father holds out his hand and shakes mine with a death grip. "A pleasure to meet you, Camryn," he says holding my gaze. It's like the words don't match his actual feelings but he's fighting his instincts to show me how he truly feels.

"Nice to meet you, too," I reply as Fletcher tugs me back to his side. I'm not sure if he's using me as a protective shield or if I'm using him as one.

"Shall we go to brunch at Mo's or are we having bagels here?" his mother asks as she eyes the bagels that have somehow magically appeared on the kitchen island. Clearly, communication is a weak point for the McDowell family.

"I wanted to check on the new store. Why don't we go to that restaurant over by it," his father says. "Your grandparents can join us and meet your girlfriend," he adds. He doesn't exactly emphasize *girlfriend*, but I feel like he does.

"On it," Dalton says as he pulls out his phone. "Gran Ha, can you and Pop meet us at the restaurant over by Al's place? In like"—he covers the phone mic and looks at his parents and, without a conversation, nods at his father—"thirty minutes? Great. See you then."

He puts his phone back in his pocket.

"I guess let's roll out," Spencer suggests. Everyone makes their way to the front door and then we smush into the elevator before I have time to consider my wardrobe or whether I can get Drew to call me with an emergency that gets me out of this incredibly awkward situation.

Fletcher's hand is on the small of my back, making little comforting circles but I am a ball of nerves. Under the best circumstances, meeting the parents seems nerve-wracking but this...this is truly a nightmare situation.

We pile into a limo that is parked out front. Everyone is talking and I'm just sitting there like Fletcher's accessory.

Eventually, Christine turns to me. "So, tell me all about you," she says, and she seems honestly interested. Have I misjudged this entire family? Possibly. I mean, Al is friends with Fletcher's grandfather. Oh shit, I'm about to meet him, too.

I rattle on about my family and schooling for the one minute that it takes. And then we are pulling up near my apartment building. I step out and two things happen at once.

My phone buzzes with a text and Hutch comes galivanting out of the woods excitedly waving his camera.

I look down and see a text from Drew.

Drew: Uh, so, your parents just dropped by with Winston.

They just got back in town and wanted to grab lunch with you. I told them there was a coffee emergency and you had to talk with a vendor. They are still here. What do I do? SOS

Holy fucking shitballs!

"The motion-sensor camera picked up something, but I can't tell what it is," Hutch says as he approaches me in full camo.

I can see Fletcher's entire family out of the corner of my eye and to say they are both intrigued and horrified by the Viking of a man that just ran at me is an understatement.

"Oh, uh, that's great, Hutch," I manage. Hutch looks around and nods at Fletcher.

"Hey," he mutters.

"Hello," Fletcher replies. I see Fletcher go to open his mouth probably to introduce Hutch to his family when I hear a voice.

"There she is," my dad says from the front door of the building.

No. No, no, no. This can't be happening.

"Dalton?" my brother's voice says. I turn to see Dalton and my brother, Winston, bro hugging. What in the actual fuck is happening?

"Hi, darling," my mom says as she hugs me. "Everything OK with the café?"

"What's wrong with the café?" Fletcher interjects.

"How do you know each other?" I ask Winston.

There is a burst of discussion from about every person there. I pick up something about Winston and Dalton being in the same fraternity when Dalton was a freshman and Winston a senior. How did I miss that connection when scouring the internet? And my parents are introducing themselves to Fletcher's parents. And Hutch is telling Fletcher about trying to catch the person leaving flowers on the bench every day. All of a sudden, Drew flies out of the front door and stops in his tracks.

"Oh, great. You found her," he says and gives me a small *I'm sorry* shrug. I glare at him.

"It's settled, then, we'll all go together," Eddie McDowell states.

"You kids got here quickly," an older woman says as she emerges from the building, followed by Al and another older man. She eyes me up and smiles broadly. "This must be Camryn."

And just like that, I'm pretty sure I have met Fletcher's entire family. Dear God, I don't know if I can survive this brunch.

"Blink twice if you are not dying of a stroke," Fletcher whispers in my ear.

"I don't think I can," I reply.

He wraps an arm around me. "Well, this is one way to rip off a bandage," he says as we assess the large group of our family members and friends.

"Not funny," I hiss.

He chuckles. "It's a little funny."

I glare at him, and he smirks. "Come on, it can't be that bad."

I hope he's right.

CHAPTER TWENTY-SIX

Fletch

"Why are they all getting along?" Cam whispers as she looks around the room. Al somehow talked Joe into letting us use his party room at the tavern down the street. And all our parents, brothers, Drew, and Al are here eating brunch with us. Hutch would have joined us but he was too keen to see what he caught on his motion-sensor camera. Everyone is talking and enjoying each other's company like old friends. My grandmother has been asking Cam a thousand questions, and Cam has politely answered each one. I can tell they like each other and that gives me some deep feelings that I'm not sure I'm ready to think about yet.

"I haven't the foggiest," I agree.

"Do you think we can sneak out of here and they won't notice?" she asks.

I give her a raised eyebrow.

"I really do have things I should get done today. Hugh told me he fixed my cooling rack, but I want to check, and Amber was able to pop in this morning and do some prep work on dough for this week. I really need to hire a second part-time person to help when Adriana is off," she rattles on with her to-do list.

"I have an idea," I say in a low voice as I look around the table. Everyone has finished eating for the most part.

"Hey, sorry to cut this short, but Cam and I have some interviews to do before the show releases," I say as I stand and pull Cam's chair back. She joins me to a chorus of people asking if we can stay for a little while longer.

"No. So sorry. We really do need to get on this call. This was lovely. It was so nice meeting you all," Cam says to my family.

"Everyone is welcome back at the apartment. I can crank the heaters on the rooftop," Al offers.

"We'll leave you all to it," I say as I give my mother and grandmother a hug and cheek kiss. Cam says goodbye to her family. They aren't at all what I had pictured. They look like the stereotypical suburban family. The fact that Winston and Dalton knew each other in college amuses me. Apparently, Dalton went by D Mac and the freshmen never learned his real name, so Winston didn't realize he had known a McDowell, and I guarantee my oldest brother was too consumed by partying to have remembered some senior's's name.

But seeing Cam's parents gush over her café and her win in the competition that made it very clear how proud they are of her. I'm not sure why she feels so much pressure to impress them.

We walk back to Cam's apartment in silence. When we reach the front door, Cam looks up at me.

"That was..." She trails off and tilts her head to the side as if considering her words.

"Fun?" I ask.

She laughs. "Traumatic?" she corrects.

I nudge her arm with mine. "Come on, it wasn't that bad."

She shakes her head. "It was that bad. We haven't even

had a real date and our entire families just met. It's like...*Alice in Wonderland*. Everything is backwards and strange and..." She pauses. "Don't you feel like we're doing this all wrong?"

Now it's me shaking my head. "No. We're doing this just right. We are building something between us. There's not a playbook or directions. We're building our own romance, Camryn. As long as it works for us, fuck everything else," I say as I pull her to me and lean down, ghosting my lips over hers. "I like our backwards, down-the-rabbit-hole relationship." I kiss her and she smiles against my lips.

"Why do grown-ups always kiss in front of the building?" Ava's voice rings out from above us.

We both look up and see her leaning out the window.

"Ava! Get back inside!" Cam yells.

"Only if you come see my new dollhouse," she bargains. Cam groans and I smirk. This kid is hilarious.

"Ava Louise Maxwell! So help me God. Your mom and I are going to have a long chat," Camryn yells.

"Please, Miss Cam. You can even bring...what's your name again?" Ava asks me.

"Fletcher," I reply.

"Mr. Fletcher can come, too. And I totally won't tell my mom about that time you let me stay up late and watch that scary movie," Ava adds.

Cam leans her forehead against my chest. "You want to come with me to see a dollhouse?" she asks.

I press my lips together to keep myself from smiling. "Sure," I manage.

I follow her inside and up the stairs. I see Ava standing at a door and she ushers us inside.

"Miss Cornelia, I'm having friends over," she says as she takes our hands and drags us past a half-asleep Cornelia in the living room. She's facing away from us and watching some reality show. "Ava, you're supposed to be napping and I'm pretty sure Cam and Fletcher don't want to play."

I raise my eyebrows and Cam laughs. "We'll just be a minute, Cornelia."

"How does she know?" I ask.

"She was a teacher. I think that *eyes in the back of the head* thing lasts forever," Cam explains as we enter a very purple room.

"I'm guessing purple is your favorite color?" I ask Ava.

"No. My favorite color is black because it has all colors, but Mom won't let me paint my room black," Ava explains. "Purple is my second favorite color."

"Right," I state as I look around. She has a dollhouse on a small table and starts to explain who each little doll is in the house. But something catches my eye. Something that everyone in this building has been looking for and no one has found. A small telephone-shaped saltshaker.

I walk over to where it sits next to a doll. "Ava, what's this?" I ask as I pick it up. Cam's still facing the dollhouse.

"Oh, I found that in the hallway by Miss Cam and Mr. Drew's apartment. Holly Dolly uses it to call her friend Mable Myrtle," Ava explains as if it's the most obvious thing in the world.

"What's that?" Cam asks as she turns and then her gaze falls on the saltshaker in my hand. She rushes over and picks it up, examining it.

"Where'd you find it?" Cam asks.

"I just said the hallway," Ava says, clearly annoyed we aren't paying more attention to her dollhouse.

"Outside my apartment?" Cam asks.

Ava nods.

Cam looks over at me and grins. "I must have dropped it when I was carrying stuff upstairs for happy hour. We made margaritas one night and I brought a bunch of stuff. I'd originally packed the saltshaker but decided to bring the sea salt instead. I thought I put the saltshaker back, but it must have been in my bag and fell out," she says as she looks at it again. "I can't believe it doesn't have a chip or crack."

"Do you want it back?" Ava asks with a frown.

Cam leans down. "How about I find your dolls a better phone?" she suggests.

Ava smiles. "OK."

"Ava, I'll come play another day. Mr. Fletcher and I have some things to do," Cam explains as she walks toward the door.

"Like what? Kissing?" Ava asks. Damn, this kid is sassy.

Cam puts her hands on her hips. "Ava, so help me, if you lean out that window again, I'm going to...well, you'll be in trouble," Cam stammers.

My lips twitch. She's adorable when she's flustered.

"Yeah, yeah. Don't forget about the new phone," Ava says.

We leave with a quick goodbye to Cornelia. We make it to Cam's door and I lean down. "Now, where were we?" I ask as I kiss her. She laughs against my lips and something about today feels perfect. And it's not even over yet.

"Come on, we probably have at last fifteen minutes before Drew comes home," she teases as she pulls me into her apartment. I follow her inside and she drags me to her bedroom.

"How about a date tonight?" I ask.

She pauses as she goes to unbuckle my belt. "For real?"

"For real," I confirm.

"I like dates," she says coyly.

"Good, because I'm pretty sure I'm going to like taking you on one," I tease.

———

After dinner and a movie, I invite Cam back to my place. She protested and said it's not convenient to her café, but I insisted my driver could take her in the morning. How she gets up at four is beyond me, but I set my alarm as she goes to use the bathroom. I may have tried to get her to spend the entire weekend with me while I was buried inside her.

My phone buzzes and I look down. It's a message from Eliza.

E: OMG! I need advice, dating advice.

I laugh. My good friend Eliza is hilarious. I feel like we can talk about anything. What turned out as a weird exchange on a dating app months ago has turned into a friendship like no other.

Me: What's up?

E: So, I just started dating this guy. And I really like him, but he might have just asked me to spend the weekend with him while we were...well, you know.

I frown. Wait, what the fuck?

Me: Uh, tell me more.

E: What else is there to say? We went to Hannigan's downtown for dinner and watched some horror movie that just came out and then we...you know and when we were... you know...he asked if I would spend the entire weekend with him. Do I say yes? This was only our first date. And he's...sort of the enemy I told you about. Well, he was.

Holy fuckballs! I look toward my bathroom where Cam or Eliza or whatever her name is went five minutes ago. How is this happening? All those texts where I said how to ruin her enemy was me giving her advice on how to end my business. Holy shit! Spencer and Dalton will never believe this. They've been telling me to go out with Eliza for months now.

I contemplate what to do and decide I shouldn't tell her yet. I don't want it to be weird. I'll have to figure out a way to tell her...later.

Me: Say yes. YOLO.

Eliza: Of course you'd say that.

Me: (smiling emoji)

Eliza: Fine, but if I have a horrible time, I'm blaming you.

Me: What if you have a great time?

Eliza: Then that was all me. (sticking-tongue-out emoji)

I grin. This is going to be fun.

CHAPTER TWENTY-SEVEN

Cam

I roll over and stare at a sleeping Fletcher. A weekend turned into two weeks. Drew has asked me repeatedly when I plan on coming home or if we're heading out to Las Vegas to get married at a chapel with a singing Elvis impersonator.

I get up and grab my phone. Heading to Fletcher's kitchen to make coffee in his professional-grade machine. I can't believe he has the same one I have at the café in his freaking kitchen.

It's three forty-five in the morning. I set my alarm extra early so I can text Max back. I set my phone on the island while I wait for the coffee machine to do its thing.

I look down and see my apartment group chat has been busy since I last checked.

Hutch: I had Kasen double-check the video I got. It might be a person, but it also might be a deer ass. I can't tell. Kasen's sending it out to some friends to see if they can make it less grainy.

Bray: For the love of all things, can you just let it go?

Hutch: NEVER!

Carly: Mr. Wilkins down at one-oh-one, says he heard that someone saw Mr. Kennison out by the bench before sunrise.

Roxy: Well, I heard from Mrs. Gansely that Mrs. Hubbins saw Mr. Totley walking by there with Mrs. Garrison. But that was like at ten something yesterday morning.

Gray: I'm on Team For the Love of All Things. Seriously, why do we care?

Hutch: Because we need answers.

Gray: (eye-rolling emoji)

Bray: (forehead-slapping emoji)

Drew: The real question is why none of Hutch's motion-sensor cameras are working properly. Like, dude, seriously, send that shit back.

Al: You kids crack me up.

Margie: They really do. It's so sweet. But I also really want to know.

Cornelia: Have we ever considered the person doesn't live around here?

Hutch: Yep. That's theory number twelve.

Jessa: We have a theory numbered list?

Troy: Jess – did you miss that happy hour?

Jessa: I guess so.

I giggle and then slap a hand over my mouth, trying to be quiet.

I hear the coffee machine start and I get out milk to froth. I glance down and see a missed text from Kasen. I frown. Kasen doesn't text that often. I click on it and go through some encryption app and read.

Kasen: My friend Jack came through. I'm sending you an encrypted text chain between the McDowell brothers now. I will say the text chain discussions about you end abruptly a few days ago. They were looking for ways to get information from you and close the café. That was part of why Fletcher was at the competition. Tread carefully, Cam.

What?

I click on a link from Kasen and go through another encryption app and then finally see a string of text messages. I read and read, and I feel myself growing angrier by the minute. What the fuck?

He's correct. All discussions about me stop right after the competition ended. Does that mean he got what he needed? Is he leading me on? What the hell?

Memories of all the sweet things he's done for me over the past two weeks flood my mind like a tsunami. Was any of this real?

I see one last missed message. Max. We've been texting off and on over the past two weeks. He keeps telling me that Fletcher sounds like *the one*. Usually Max is right.

Max: I'm serious, E. I know you two had a rocky start, but give him a chance. It sounds like he's trying to figure out a way you both can succeed in your businesses and stay together. That's not an easy feat. I still think you should give him a chance. People change, E.

I roll my eyes. Right. People change. I'm an idiot.

I dump my half-drunk coffee into the sink and place the mug in the dishwasher. Part of me, the immature part, wants to leave it all out. He does have staff that clean.

I tiptoe into the bedroom and grab my bag from Fletcher's closet. I'm done playing games. Why wouldn't he have just told me this? If he's hiding it from me, he must still be trying to get information from me. I mean, I was trying to get information from him too, but that was before the competition. He was still texting during the competition.

I frown as I consider this, but in the end, I decide I can't trust him. I take my clothes off hangers and out of the one drawer I've been using these last two weeks. I grab my toiletries from the bathroom, and I take one final look at the sleeping Fletcher McDowell. He's on his back, his perfect abs on full display. I hate that he's so gorgeous.

I turn on my heels and head out the door and away from this man who I clearly can't trust. A small part of me feels a pang of guilt. Maybe I should have spoken with him. No, I did teasingly tell him last week that I was trying to find a way to rebrand myself differently than him; so I didn't lie about looking into his company. Now, I did leave out that little detail about Kasen searching them up, but that's a small detail.

The memory of last week comes back to me.

"So, how were you planning to leave my business in ruins?" he asks as we lie in bed, facing each other.

I blush. I feel like an idiot. "I was snooping around trying to figure out how you were going to brand, so I could do something different," I admit.

"Oh, did you figure that out?" he asks, taking a strand of my hair and wrapping it around his finger.

"No, but don't think I won't keep trying," I tease as I poke his chest. He tugs on my hair, and I scoot closer to him.

"We aren't going to have to worry about that anymore," he assures me.

"No?" I ask as I press my lips to his.

"No, Tanner. There's no more competition between us, except in how well we can please each other in bed," he replies with a laugh and tickles me. "Come here, Hollywood."

"Why Hollywood?" I question with a grin.

"You're going to be famous with the show airing. You were a natural behind the camera," he explains.

I laugh and he rolls me underneath me.

Was his statement about not competing anymore because

they have a plan to put me out of business? I scowl at my own stupidity. I shouldn't have trusted him.

———

I leave Adriana to close. She's showing my new employee, Julie, the ropes. I can't believe I hired another employee.

I wave bye and walk across the street with my bag slung on my shoulder. I look down and see a dozen missed texts from Fletcher.

Fletcher: Where's your stuff?

Fletcher: You know you can use my washer and dryer.

Fletcher: Cam. What's going on?

Missed call from Fletcher.

Fletcher: Answer me!

Fletcher: I'm so pissed right now. You better answer me!

Fletcher: Cam, please answer!

Fletcher: ???

Another missed call from Fletcher.

Fletcher: I'm texting Drew.

Fletcher: Can you at least text Drew?

Missed call from Drew.

Drew: Uh, what the fuck is up? I'm at work. Guess it's a *lime in the coconut* night.

Fletcher: Hollywood, please call me.

Fletcher: Cam, please call me.

Another missed call from Fletcher.

Fletcher: Damn it, Cam. I have a meeting I can't miss. I'll meet you after you close.

I sigh and shove my phone back in my pocket as I walk up to my apartment. I sling my overnight bag over my shoulder and contemplate what to do next.

I don't even get my key in the lock before Drew has the

door open. He's holding a margarita with a lime wedge and salt on the rim.

"I think you need this," he states as he takes my bag from me. I walk inside and am greeted by Carly, Piper, Roxy, Margie, Jessa, Jocelyn, and Cornelia.

I'm so tired that instead of being happy to see all my friends, I just burst into tears.

"Oh shit, I told you this was a bad idea," Cornelia says as Carly pulls me into a hug.

"N-no," I stammer as I sob. "I'm j-just tired and...why'd h-he have to be so g-great."

Carly pats my back. I pull away and wipe my eyes. I hate crying and I really hate crying in front of people.

"Sit down. It's therapy cocktail hour. Lay it on us, kid," Margie insists as she pats the sofa next to her.

I sit down and sip my margarita, letting myself take a few deep breaths. I suppose if I can't tell these ladies, and Drew, about what's happening, then who can I tell?

"Kasen found texts between Fletch and his brothers. Fletch told them he would join me at the competition, so he could spy on me and get dirt that would help them take customers from me," I explain.

"Did Kasen get any dirt on their branding plans?" Drew asks, inquiring about my original ask of Kasen.

I shake my head. "No. And you know what, I did sort of tell Fletcher that I was looking into his company, but he never once mentioned spying on me. If he had been upfront, then maybe I wouldn't have cared so much, but this...it just felt like...I couldn't trust him anymore." I sigh. "I've worked so hard to get the café up and running how I want it. I really wanted to show Winston and my parents how far I've come and that I can do this. Then, I was going to focus on dating once I had the business set. But like an idiot, I jump in bed with the first guy I've connected with in over a year." I groan at my stupidity.

Margie pats my shoulder. "Well, at least you figured it out now and not on your wedding night, dear."

I glance over at her. "Uh, sure."

"I found out my husband had been the town whore on our wedding night. That was eye-opening," she says with a sigh.

"Oh, don't listen to Margie. She was a big prude back then. Maybe Fletcher *was* going to tell you. Men are slow sometimes. You could give him a chance to explain himself," Cornelia suggests.

I shake my head and drink more margarita. "I need some time to think about all of this."

Jocelyn peers out the window. "Uh, I think your time is up. Fletcher just got out of a car and is walking up to the café."

Shit. "Can we move this party to someone else's place?" I ask. The last thing I need is to create a big scene in front of them all when Fletcher inevitably shows up at my door.

"Come on," Margie says, standing and holding out her hand for me. I take it and we all walk to her and Cornelia's apartment.

Drew stays at the door and I look back at him. "I'll talk to him. I'll be up shortly," he assures me.

"Thank you," I say as I hug him. He hugs my back.

"I'd do anything for you, kid," he whispers. I feel tears threaten again because I wish it was Fletcher saying those words. I'm so pissed off at him. I was beginning to trust him, really trust him. And then Kasen had to show me those text messages. I've had boyfriends cheat on me in the past, and somehow, this feels the same if not worse.

It hits me like a ton of bricks as I pull away. The reason I'm so upset over a relationship that is only a month old is that I have fallen for Fletcher. That's why I'm so upset. Damn it! I can't believe I gave my heart away so easily. Never again. I'm about to go on a man-hiatus. No more men. No more Fletcher.

CHAPTER TWENTY-EIGHT

Fletch

She wasn't at the café. She's not answering my calls or emails. What the fuck?

We made love last night. I've all but confessed that I'm falling in love with her. Everything was great. And now, she's ghosting me? I don't understand.

I knock on her door and Drew opens it. I step back because this man looks like he's about to rearrange my face.

I put my hands up in defense. "I don't know what's going on, but I swear I didn't intentionally do anything to hurt her," I start.

He snarls at me. "Really? Is that so?" Drew asks, crossing his arms. His biceps bulge and for a split second I want to ask what gym the guys in this building go to because they all look like they could take down the most hardened criminal. And I have a feeling Drew might try his left hook on me if I don't figure out how to explain whatever it is that he thinks I did, that apparently Camryn thinks I did.

"I have no idea what's going on. Everything was going great and then she left this morning and took all her stuff," I explain.

Drew sighs. "You are sort of an idiot, you know that?" he asks as he steps aside and motions for me to come into the apartment.

I look around him to make sure I'm not going to get ambushed, but he appears to be alone.

I hesitantly step inside, and he shuts the door.

"Did you get what you needed from her?" he asks as he leans with his back against a wall.

"Get what from her? I don't understand. Whatever rivalry we had, it's done, over," I state.

He raises an eyebrow. "Over? Really," he says, his voice laced with sarcasm.

"Listen, are you going to explain what's happening here or am I going to have to park myself on your sofa until Camryn comes here to tell me herself," I say with a challenging raise of my eyebrow.

"You fucking plotted with your brothers to get intel on her café so you could figure out how to take her customers and drive her out of business. And then you just *failed* to mention that to her after you called a *truce*?" he asks, waving a hand in the air as if to say, *see*.

"I-I was, but...that was weeks ago, before we won the competition. Before I..." I trail off, not wanting to put all my cards on the table for Drew to see.

"Before you what?" Drew asks, narrowing his eyes.

I sigh and turn to the window, looking out at her café. The lights are off now. I look at the business next door, the one I just bought, the one I was secretly hoping to use to add to the café's size. My plan, the one I've spent two weeks trying to work out is to sell the McDowell's current spot to a chef friend of mine and instead act as a silent minority partner in Cam's Café. My concept is that McDowell's can partner with smaller bakeries and cafés to broaden our portfolio while helping small businesses. I'd be Cam's partner, not her enemy. I could fund all the great ideas she's talked about as we lie in bed at night. We could make the greatest neighborhood café ever. And if my family vetoes the idea, then I'm prepared to step away from it all and invest my own money in the café. I've already used my own funds to buy the place next door and I'm prepared to buy out the building leasing the café space. We could own the whole thing. I know with the show starting next week, Cam's Café is going to see a huge uptick in its business. It's the perfect time to invest. If I don't, I bet someone else will. And no one is going to care more about helping her than me.

I put my thumbs in my pockets. Fuck it! I'll put all my cards on the table. If anyone can talk sense into my woman, it's Drew.

"Before I fell in love with her," I admit, not turning around to see his reaction.

But I hear it. A single sharp intake of breath.

"You *love* her?" he repeats.

I nod. "I don't know when it happened. She pissed me the hell off. She drove me nuts. And then...somewhere between saving her from a spider at the hotel and taking her on a real date, I fell for her. I don't want to shut down the café," I state as I turn to Drew. "I want to expand it." I let out a long breath. I haven't even told my family yet, but I have to tell him or he won't believe me. "I bought the building next door and I offered to buy the building where the café is located. The dry cleaners was going out of business and the building's owner wanted to sell. So, I bought it. I want to be a silent minority partner in Cam's company. I want to invest capital, let her do all the great ideas she has. I believe in her business. I want to see it grow. I've already talked to a chef friend who wants to buy the McDowell property for a sandwich shop. I think it'll do really well in this neighborhood," I explain. I meet his gaze. He's eyeing me with suspicion. I can see him warring over whether he should trust me or not.

I put my hands up in surrender. "I love her, Drew. I don't want to hurt her. I'm not sure what she saw to think I want to ruin her business, but that's not how I feel any longer. She even admitted to essentially spying on me to get intel. We were doing the same thing," I offer.

He rolls his eyes. "Yeah, but she admitted it and you never said fuck all."

I grimace. He's right. I just felt stupid at that point. "You're right. I should have told her. I just figured...it's water under the bridge. What's the point of telling her something that I sort of figured she'd already know."

"You sort of figured wrong, bro," Drew says deadpan.

"Yeah, I see that now. I'm an idiot, but I'm an idiot that's fucking head over heels in love with her," I lament.

I pull an envelope from my pocket. I had grabbed it this morning. I wanted to show it to her in person.

I pass it to him, and he opens it, reading the copy of the deed and my business plan. Then he passes it back to me.

"How do I know that's true and not some made-up shit?" he asks.

I pull up my email and hold up my phone, showing him email chains with a realtor and the building's owner. Then I show him call logs and play two voicemails. By the time I play the second one, he holds up his hand.

"She had Kasen try to get her intel on your company while you were attempting to do the same to hers. He got it, but after you all shacked up for two weeks. He sent it anyhow and I guess she didn't know what to believe. She thought you might still want to put her out of business. She's had douchebags do stupid shit to her before, so she doesn't give trust easily. I think she felt like an idiot that was getting taken advantage of. You really fucked up by not telling her what you were doing sooner. Anyhow, you both suck at communicating and need to work on that shit," Drew says.

I shrug. He's not wrong. "So, how do I fix it? Where is she?" I ask, looking around.

"Elsewhere. You won't be able to talk to her tonight. You need a real plan." He pauses and looks at his watch and then grins. "I'm late for a meeting. And you're coming with me."

———

"Classic mistake right there," Hutch says with a laugh. He snaps his fingers. "It's like that one enemies to lovers we read three months ago. What was the name of it? Anyhow, you all fell in love but also secretly were still suspect of each other because it all happened too fast. The enemies part was blurring with the lovers part. And you suck at communication."

I groan. "Yeah, sort of already heard that tonight. How do I fix it, then?"

"Grand gesture," Kasen says as he leans back. "You fucked up, bro. Your girl is as headstrong as they come. Also, next time you text shit, just remember, anyone can get that. I don't care that you were on your company's super secure chat app. You all didn't even encrypt it, novice fucking mistake."

I glare at him. He's the reason my woman is mad at me, and I sort of want to beat the shit out of him.

He smirks. "Cam is going to need the biggest grand gesture ever. She's stubborn as fuck."

Sighing, I nod. "I know. Trust me, I know."

"Well, what's your plan?" Drew asks.

I stand and walk in a circle as ideas roll around my brain. "I'm going to need two weeks and a lot of help," I finally say as the perfect plan starts to form in my mind.

Drew looks to Bray, Gray, Hutch, and Kasen. "We're in."

I smile. "Time to do some epic shit. If I can't win her back with this, then...well, I guess I don't deserve her."

Drew gives me a stern look. "No one deserves her. She's too good for any of us. But I think you both are in love with each other and I'm all for an old-fashioned love story. So, let's go help you win back your lady." He pauses. "Prepare for a lot of groveling. She's a...well, she's Cam."

They chuckle and give me looks of sympathy. But that only invigorates me. My lady is as headstrong as they come and that's going to make this even more worthwhile when I prove to her how much I love her. Holy fuck, I love Camryn Tanner!

CHAPTER TWENTY-NINE

Cam

"What the hell is this?" I ask as I look at Drew's phone. He just asked me to grab it for him and I see a text message notification from Vito, his ex.

"What's what?" he asks, wiping his hands on his apron as he makes us BLTs on fresh bread. Drew's grandfather loved to cook, and where I'm the baker, Drew is an all-around chef. We make a good pair. Maybe I'm destined to be single forever and I get Drew instead of a boyfriend. I suppose there are far worse fates than getting to live with your best friend, even if that means no sex.

I hold up the phone and his eyes widen. He sets down a pair of tongs on the counter and turns to me.

"Don't be mad, but I started messaging with Vito a few weeks ago," he starts.

"You what? And you didn't think to tell me this?" I ask. Not only am I shocked, I'm also hurt that he didn't mention it.

"I'm sorry. I had a moment of weakness when you were with *He Who Shall Not Be Named* and I was lonely and I had one too many martinis at happy hour and I sort of messaged him. I was a little surprised when he messaged back and then we just started talking again. I wanted to tell you but then you broke it off with Fletcher and I felt bad being like, *oh, hey, me and my ex might get back together*, when you are freshly single again. I was going to tell you in a few more weeks," he explains.

"So, are you two back together?" I ask.

He shrugs. "I might fly over there for a visit and just see how things go. We're going to take it slow this time. He's working for a big corporation that has an office in Rome."

I step forward and wrap my arms around him, pulling him in for a hug. "I'm happy for you. Vito is a really good guy. I hope you guys can work it out."

And even though I'm jealous as fuck, I truly am happy for Drew. He deserves the world.

"You know, you could try talking to Fletcher," he says against my hair. I pull away and scoff at him.

"No way. What's the point? He stopped texting me a few days ago. I think he's given up trying and I'm tired of worrying about whether he actually is trustworthy or if he is still an asshole. How can we build a relationship when I can't trust him?" I ask, but really I'm asking myself.

"What if you can trust him?" Drew questions.

I shrug.

"I think you at least owe him a conversation," he says. "If you're going to end things, then woman up and end them face to face."

I hate that he's right. I probably do at least owe him a conversation. I've managed to ghost him for almost two weeks. Albeit I've been busy. The building next door is going through renovations. I'm training our new staff and I'm trying to stay more in the back and let Adriana and Julie handle the front. That at least keeps me from prying eyes.

Sighing, I lean against our counter. "You're right. I guess I'll text him or something. I just...what if he's all sweet and then sucks me back in," I say.

Drew laughs. "You mean, what if you were wrong and he's actually a good guy?"

I glare at my best friend, and he laughs some more. "I swear, you are so stubborn to spite yourself at times. You know, couples do fight sometimes and then they make up and life goes on."

I shrug again. "But seriously, let's look at it objectively. We are so different. He's a rich playboy. I'm from a normal family and I know I haven't been with as many men as he's been with women," I state.

"OK, so you come from different backgrounds. You both like baking. You both like running businesses. You both like family and friends. Those are all big things," he points out and I sort of hate that he's not wrong.

"I guess," I reply. The more Drew talks, the more I start to wonder if I overreacted.

"Drew?"

"Yes, toots," he says, going back to flipping bacon.

"What if...what if I fucked it up and it's too late?" I whisper.

He glances over at me. "Then, you'll move on and find someone even better. But don't underestimate Fletcher. You never know, he could be the one."

I laugh. "OK, oh wise one."

He winks. "I know. I can't help it."

I throw a towel at him, and we finish making dinner, him cooking and me setting the table. But Drew's statement about Fletcher being the one keeps playing in my mind. What if Drew is right? I guess I'll call Fletcher tomorrow. I need to build up some bravery first.

————

I stare at my phone. I've put it across my desk so I'm not tempted to look at it. I texted Fletcher earlier and am waiting to see if he replies.

Did I overreact? Possibly. OK, fine, I probably overreacted. I should have at least let him explain himself.

I sigh. My worst trait is a tie between being stubborn and overreacting.

Did I really get that close to having it all and then throw it in the trash all because of a possible miscommunication?

I check my messages from Max. He's been my lifeline these past two weeks. I wish we weren't such good friends, I'd tell him we should try dating. I see a missed message from him, and I smile for the first time today.

Max: Hey, E. I'm sorry he hasn't responded to you. Maybe he's still hurt and needs some time?

Me: Maybe. But it's been almost two weeks. The building next door has had around-the-clock construction which is super annoying. I can't find the owner to complain. I'm supposed to be doing last-minute media for the show and I don't know if I'll see him or not. I just don't know what to think. I feel awful that I didn't at least give him a chance to tell me his side of the story. But I'm also still hurt.

Max: I know. I'm sure he'll respond to you. Give him a little more time.

Me: What if I show up at his office?

Max: I mean, that's one way to get his attention.

Me: Ugh! I hate this! I miss his stupid, annoying, sexy self. God, I'm an idiot.

Max: (laughing emoji) An adorable idiot.

Me: (middle-finger emoji)

I see a missed text from my family group chat.

Winston: Good luck today! Can't wait to see the show.

Mom: Same.

Dad: Break a leg, kid!

I laugh.

Me: Thanks. I'm excited to watch the show too.

Fletch had told me about how proud my family is of me, and I didn't see it before the past few days, but I am starting to believe him. It'll take time for me to accept that as truth. I'm so used to being the baby of the family that everyone dotes on and takes care of. Doing this on my own was to prove I can. I didn't think proving it to myself would help but I think it has. I can see my strengths now. I'm so much stronger than I thought I was. I don't need anyone, but damn, do I wish Fletcher was by my side for this wild ride. He'd be the perfect partner. I wish I knew what he was concocting before I left that morning. He kept saying he had a plan, but I don't know what that plan was.

"Felicity is here to set up for the media shoot later," Adriana calls out from the front.

"Coming," I say as I shut down my laptop and straighten my desk for the tenth time today. The network wanted to do some last-minute media blitzing and that includes an interview with me at the café. She had mentioned asking Fletcher to be here too, but she later told me he was busy and we'd do interviews with him later.

Part of me feels a pang in my chest at the thought of going another day without talking to him. I keep wanting to share things with him, a new recipe I made a few days ago, a funny horror movie I watched with Drew, and even a new special shelf in my office for the saltshaker so that I never lose it again. Carly may have apologized a dozen times about that, although it's completely not anyone's fault. I'm just glad we found it.

I decide to send him one more text before I go out front.

Me: I don't know if you're reading my texts, but I hope you are. I know I can do this on my own, but it'd be so much better if you were here beside me. I miss you and I'm sorry. I hope someday you'll forgive me.

I push my phone into my signature apron pocket with my new Cam's Café logo on it and walk out front. I wish the giant hole in the side of the café was repaired. Apparently, our building manager found an internal wiring issue when the building next door had to tear down part of the wall. We were closed for two days, but fortunately there was a local indoor, holiday farmer's market nearby and we were able to set up a table there and sell some items.

I haven't seen the damage yet as Gregor, the building owner, had the contractor curtain off the section of wall that's being replaced. It's huge and takes up nearly forty percent of the wall. But it'll get fixed and at least I don't have to pay for it. As Drew pointed out, I can use this as an opportunity to rebrand with new paint and new artwork. We came up with our plan a few days ago and have all the paint ready to go once I get the green light. I was a little bummed that the building next door sold. I had thought about trying to lease that space to expand the café.

I hate filming in here without it being updated, but Felicity was insistent that we get it done today.

I enter the main part of the café. My staff are lined up behind the counter. The film crew is set up and there's a small bistro table in the light, which I assume is where I'll be sitting.

"Oh, wonderful, you're ready," Felicity says as she claps her hands together. Outside the door, I see my neighbors clustered around the front window, watching us.

I laugh and wave to them. They all wave back.

I look around again, a small part of me hoping to see Fletcher, but he's nowhere to be seen. I glance at the offending curtain. It's still there.

"Camryn, this is Wendy Belden. She'll be interviewing you," Felicity introduces the woman already seated on one side of the bistro table. I recognize her from a news program that follows restaurants and chefs.

I hold out my hand to her and she shakes it. "It's a pleasure to meet you," she says. "Shall we get started?"

I nod and sit down. After the three-person crew gets organized, we start the interview. She asks the same questions I've already heard from other press during our initial press tour a few weeks ago. I wonder why we were even doing this.

"And what are your plans moving forward now that you've won?" she asks as her questions begin to indicate that we are wrapping up the interview.

"Well, I'd love to expand a bit if the opportunity arises. And I have ideas for some new menu items; those are already in the works. I also have some new visual changes I'd like to make here at the café," I answer as I give her my best fake smile which I've been perfecting.

"That's wonderful," she answers and then gives me a real smile. I'm not used to that, an interviewer giving me a genuine smile is unusual to say the least. "What if I told you we had a little surprise for you today?"

I raise my eyebrows. "Oh?"

She grins. "Mr. McDowell, would you like to join us?" she says loudly.

All of a sudden, the curtains that were stapled over the opening in my wall are ripped down and Fletcher is standing in what looks like giant double doors. He pushes them back and I realize the store next to mine that's been under renovation is now connected to my café.

I frown. What in the actual hell is happening?

"Hey," he says. "Sorry it took me so long to get back to you, but I've sort of been scrambling to get something done."

I look around him at the store on the other side. It looks like the exact replica of what Drew and I dreamed up over drinks less than a week ago. How in the hell did he do that?

I'm baffled and speechless.

He walks over to me and offers me his hand. It takes me a moment but I hesitantly accept it. He pulls me to my feet and leans down a little so we are nose to nose.

"I'm not sorry Kasen sent you my texts, albeit I'm not pleased with his methods, but I would have told you myself eventually. I just didn't know how to explain that I've changed. When you wouldn't answer me, I may have ended up talking to Drew and some of your other friends. I decided I needed really big actions not just words. Remember a few weeks ago when we...were hanging out and you told me about your dreams for the café?" he asks.

I nod a little, keeping my gaze on his. "Well, I decided I want to be part of your dream. I sold the McDowell's property down the street to my chef friend. He's opening a sandwich shop there in a few weeks. And I talked the owner of the building next door and perhaps Gregor into selling their buildings to me. And with the second sale being official today, we can expand Cam's Café just like you wanted. I used all the information Drew sent me and we can finish this side now that I've got the other side done. We'll need to connect the kitchens, but this more than doubles your front space and nearly doubles your back space. I want to be your silent partner, your silent minority partner. You will maintain majority rule in the company. I'm going to provide capital and assistance where you need it to make your café a success. I think it's a really good start," he explains and pauses. "If that's alright with you, of course."

"Really?" I ask because the words coming out of his mouth feel like a dream and not reality.

He nods and rubs his nose against mine. "There is one other small problem."

I crinkle my nose. "What's that?"

"I may need to move in with you," he says, and my eyes widen further.

"I'm sorry, what?"

"I left McDowell's. Well, I'm creating my own sub-company under the McDowell's umbrella that partners with smaller cafés and bakeries and you're my first partnership, I mean, if you accept," he explains.

"I don't understand," I say.

"I forgive you and I'm sorry you saw those texts. I sold my condo to pay for these buildings because I wanted to do this on my own. I'm living upstairs in office space right now and I could really use a nicer place," he says.

"What? Why would you do that?" I ask, pulling back a little. Everyone else in the room has faded away and right now all I see is Fletcher.

He licks his lips, and I can tell he's nervous, but am not sure why.

"Because, Camryn Eliza Tanner, I'm in love with you and I want to do this with you, not against you, not competing with you, just...with you, you and me," he says, pointing between us.

I freeze when he says my middle name. I've never told him that.

"How did you...why do you know my middle name?" I whisper. Somewhere, deep, deep down I start to put pieces of a puzzle together and hope blooms in my chest. What if the two men I've adored for months are in fact the same person? No, that can't be. That's crazy. Things like that don't happen, not in the real world. Those things happen in fiction, in the romance books across the street.

"Because, my middle name is Maxwell or…Max," he says with a wink. "Not sure how you didn't put that together before."

"No," I say. How did I not think about that? I do remember seeing his middle named when I stalked him on the internet, but I never imagined he would go by Max on a dating app.

He nods. "Yes."

"No fucking way," I state.

"Yes fucking way, Hollywood, or should I say Eliza?" he says with a slight smirk.

"It's been you this whole time?" I ask.

He nods again. "I might have figured it out the night you told me about where you went on the date," he admits.

I slap my forehead. "Oh my God! I've told you…like, so many personal things." I lower my voice as I feel a blush creep across my cheeks. "Like really, really personal things."

He grins. "You have. So you see, we may have just started dating about…" He looks down at his watch. "Six-ish weeks ago, but we've been talking for over six months."

"I can't believe this is happening," I whisper.

"What do you say? Drew's already down with it," he adds, nodding his head to motion toward the window where Drew is holding up a sign that says, "Say Yes, Beotch."

I giggle and bite my lip as I consider everything. I'm so overwhelmed.

As if sensing this, Fletcher cups my face in his hands. "You and me, we got this. We make the perfect team, E. Please give us a chance."

I search his eyes and all I see is my future, our future. We'll build a life together and it'll be perfect. It'll be everything I ever wanted and more.

"OK," I whisper. "You win."

He grins against my lips. "I win?"

I nod. "Yeah, are you going to close this deal with a kiss or what?"

He chuckles. "Always," he whispers back as he presses his lips to mine.

CHAPTER THIRTY

Fletch

"There's no way it's all fitting in there," Cam says.

"That's what she said!" Drew yells from the other room.

"Well, it has to go somewhere," I state as I look at the closet. It's a walk-in but it's probably a quarter of the size of my walk-in closet. I still can't believe I sold my condo. I have half thought about kicking the residents out of the apartments over Cam's Café, but the legality of doing it is a nightmare and Cam has repeatedly said if I do that, we are over.

Yet right now, it sounds tempting.

"Don't even think about it," she says as she stares at me.

"I mean, we could turn one whole apartment into a giant closet," I point out. I still have most of my things in storage. I know this living situation isn't going to be permanent, but for now, I have to figure out how it will work. Cam has told me there is no way she's moving and there's no way I'm ending leases early across the street. Eventually, I have plans for a two-floor condo above our café, complete with rooftop deck.

She puts her hands on her hips and glares at me. I laugh and pull her to me, kissing the tip of her nose.

"I'm kidding," I state.

She leans against me and puts her head in the crook of my neck. I hold her tightly.

"Ewww! Get a room," Drew calls out from the hallway.

"We are already in a room," Cam retorts.

"OK, I mean, that's fair," he replies and then pops his head in the doorway. "I have news, by the way."

Cam peels her head from my neck and looks over at him. "What's that?"

"Come to happy hour. I want to tell everyone together," he says.

She frowns and looks up at me. "What's going on?" she asks as she steps out of my embrace and toward Drew.

"It's all good. I just have happy news," he announces.

"Don't I get bestie intel first?" she pouts, pushing out her bottom lip.

"You sort of won't be surprised about it. We've spoken about it, generally," he teases.

"I hate you," she grumbles.

"Love you too, pookie bear," he says making an air kiss.

Cam rolls her eyes. "You two are driving me insane. I'm going to go check on the café. I'll meet you at happy hour."

We just finished the rest of the construction work and plan to reopen on Monday. In the meantime, I bought us a small food truck that we've been serving coffee and a few pastries from out front. I didn't want Cam to lose any customers during our construction project.

"You want me to come with you?" I ask.

"No. I got it. Just want to make sure Hugh set up the new oven how I want. I'll be up in ten minutes," she assures me.

I watch as she goes and then I turn to Drew. "What's the news?"

He shrugs. "Just some love life updates."

I raise an eyebrow. "Please tell me you aren't having someone move in here."

He laughs. "Hell no. Three's company and four would be a disaster."

I chuckle. "OK. Glad we are on the same page about that."

"Completely. Now, let's get up to happy hour. I hear we have guests tonight," Drew says, and I groan. Al had promised to invite my family to happy hour last week. I pretended that was a great idea, but I have a sneaking suspicion he believed me.

I follow Drew upstairs and sure enough. My brothers are at the bar. Al has the heat lamps on and the fire pit going where Ava, Carly, and Bray are roasting marshmallows.

Everyone else is clustered around the bar and a table. There are pizzas stacked to the one side. My parents are chatting with Jessa, Troy, Margie, and Cornelia, while Hutch, Kasen, Piper, Gray, Jocelyn, and Roxy are at the bar.

"Usual?" Al calls out to us.

"Yes, please," we say in unison.

"Where's your better half?" Spencer asks.

"Checking on the new ovens," I explain as I lean against the bar.

"And then I had Kasen run it through more software but I can't tell anything and neither can he," Hutch says to Jocelyn.

"You know, you could just find another hobby," she replies as she leans closer to him. I can't help wondering if something is going on between those two. Then my eyes drift back to the fire pit. The fact that Carly and Bray aren't together is more baffling.

"But why? I'm devoted to this until I solve the mystery," he declares.

Everyone groans and my brothers give me a look that says they have no idea what the hell we're talking about.

I shake my head at them and mouth, "You don't want to know."

They shrug and go back to a conversation with Gray about a score he recently composed for a film. I'm about to ask Al if he can make Cam's drink when I feel arms wrap around my waist from behind.

I take the hand on my abdomen and bring it to my lips, kissing the back of it.

"Usual, Cam?" Al asks.

"Yep. Thanks, Al," she replies as I tug her around to my front. "Hey," she says softly once she's in front of me.

"Hey," I reply as I gaze into her eyes. I'm not sure how my life ended up changing so drastically these past few months, but I wouldn't want it any other way. I'm in charge of my own company. I'm doing something I love that doesn't involve cutthroat business decisions. I get to work with my girlfriend who I am head over heels in love with. And I somehow got an entire new group of friends. And unlike the friends I had when I was younger, these friends like me for who I am, not how much money I have.

"What?" she says as she looks up at me.

"Just happy," I admit.

She grins at me. "Me too," she whispers.

There's a clinking of a glass and everyone turns to see Drew holding up his drink. "I have an announcement," he says.

A quiet descends upon us.

"Are you getting a new bubble kit?" Ava yells from the fire pit where she's holding up a marshmallow.

Cam nearly chokes on her drink, and I pat her back.

"Nope. But I might need to get one," Drew replies. Cam coughs some more and several other people laugh. Clearly there's an inside joke here.

"What's so funny?" I whisper in her ear.

"We use bubble blowing as a term for something else and Ava obviously doesn't get it," she whispers back.

I grin and nod my understanding as we both turn back toward Drew.

"Vito and I have been talking and we're giving it another go. I'm heading over to Rome for a few weeks to see how it works out," he says.

"Wait, what?" Cam says as she steps away from me and toward Drew.

"I just want to spend a month there and see. Maybe we still have a spark and maybe we don't, you know?" he says.

She wraps her arms around his middle, and he hugs her back with one arm while his other holds his drink.

"I'm going to miss you," she groans.

"I'll miss you too, but we can video-chat every day. Heck, if you all need a break, you can come visit me," he insists.

"Wow, I can't believe you're doing it. I hope it goes well," she replies, pulling away from him and leaning back against me. I wrap my arm around her middle.

"I'm sure we'll find something to do while he's gone," I tease her. She elbows me.

But secretly, I'm excited for some alone time. Things have been so crazy that we've hardly had a break the last few weeks.

"Oh, and cheers to our new movie stars," Drew adds as he motions to the two of us.

Cam blushes and bats her hand at him. "It's just a little competition show."

"Little!" Roxy says. "It's all everyone is talking about. The media loves that you two ended up together. It's so romantic!"

I groan and Cam laughs. "Who would have thought?" she says.

"Who would have thought," I repeat.

"Cheers, beotches," Drew says and we all clink glasses.

"Mr. Drew! That's a bad word!" Ava yells.

"Thanks, Ava. I'll remember that," he replies as he drops a quarter in a jar on the bar that says, Ava's Swear Jar.

"What does the money go toward?" I ask Cam.

Cam giggles. "Ava wants a commercial bubble blower for the rooftop."

I press my lips together trying to fight my smile. "Oh," I manage. I see Roxy leaning in to explain what bubble blowing means to my brothers whose lips both start twitching into a smile.

Cam doubles over with laughter, and pretty soon everyone around us is laughing too.

"What's so funny?" Ava asks as she runs over to us with marshmallow all over her lips.

Drew is now in hysterics. "N-nothing," he manages as he wipes tears from his eyes.

"Whatever. Mr. Al, can I have another Shirley Temple?" she asks.

"Coming up, kiddo," Al replies.

I look around us, and for the first time in my life, I feel complete. I'm not sure when I built such a great life, but I wouldn't have it any other way. Cam and I have everything we need right here on this deck.

EPILOGUE

Cam

Several Weeks Later...

"The car will be here in ten minutes!" Fletcher yells from the living room. After a grand reopening last week, we are off to visit Drew and Vito. Drew has decided to stay for another month in Italy and we've decided to spend our holidays there.

My life has been such a whirlwind that I've hardly had time to contemplate everything that's happened. The café is doing amazing. The show's grand finale is in three weeks and we are having a viewing party at the café to celebrate. We've hired three new employees two weeks ago. And our profits are through the roof. I keep pinching myself.

Fletcher wants to wait and see if we can continue our success for the rest of the year, and if things are going well, he wants to invest in another small café in another city. I think he's crazy to take on more work, but I support helping small businesses, so I guess if that means he spends some time doing that, then that's what we'll do. At least now, we have enough staff that I feel confident leaving for a few days.

I stuff the last of my toiletries into my suitcase and manage to zip it closed. I drag it into the living room.

"All set," I declare.

"Who's watching the apartment?" he asks.

"Al said he'd take in the mail and Ava and Carly are going to watch things for us," I answer as I look around once more making sure I haven't forgotten anything.

I frown. "Wait. Are we doing wrapped gifts for Christmas?" I ask. Why hadn't I thought of this? Did he bring a gift? We had originally said the trip was our gift to each other. Vito's parents own a vineyard in Tuscany and we're staying at a guesthouse on the property for most of our stay and Fletcher got us first-class plane tickets.

"I might have something small for you to unwrap," he confesses.

I groan. "You suck! I'll find you something," I say as we make our way to the door and lock up.

We take the elevator down, which was pre-agreed upon since we almost never use it.

We get outside and I see a limo pulling up. Of course, he got a limo.

"The only gift I need is you," he says, pulling me against him and kissing me.

"Ewww!" Ava calls out from above us.

"Ava, so help me, if you are leaning out that window!" I yell. That kid is going to be the death of all of us.

"Nope. Not leaning out," she says.

We both look up and only see her head.

"Have fun on your trip," she says.

"We will," we reply in unison. I look down the street and see Jocelyn talking to Hutch at the bench. He hands her the bench flowers, and she giggles.

"What's up with those two?" Fletcher asks as the driver loads our bags into the limo.

"No idea. But there's definitely some sparks between them, right?" I say as I crawl into the warm car interior and out of the gently falling snow.

"That there is," Fletcher agrees, scooting in beside me. He pulls me against him, and I lean on his shoulder.

"We are not talking shop on this trip," I state.

"No shop. But we are going to some really great bakeries," he points out.

"Fine. We can taste-test, but no buying stores or entering competitions or anything," I say.

"I can probably agree to that," he replies. I elbow him and he laughs.

"Fine, we will take a proper vacation," he agrees.

I look up at him and then down at his lap.

"Eros," I state.

He throws his head back and laughs. "How'd you figure it out?"

I shrug. "He's like the god of love, right?"

Fletcher nods.

"It's fitting," I declare, and he gives me a smug smile. I roll my eyes and he laughs again.

I lean my head back down and he wraps his arm more tightly around my shoulders.

"I love you," he whispers as the driver gets into the car.

"I love you more," I reply back.

"Not possible," he replies.

"Is too," I retort.

"We'll see about that, Hollywood," he teases, and I sigh with contentment against him. I don't think we'll ever stop competing, but I wouldn't have it any other way. When I decided to buy the café, I knew I could build a great bakery. What I didn't realize is that I'd be building an entire life I never imagined was possible. Yet here I am, looking out at the city's number one café while leaning on the shoulder of the most perfect man in the world while heading out to see one of my amazing friends. I dare say, I'm proud of this big life I've built. And I can't wait to see what comes next.

I hope you enjoyed this story. Ready for Hutch's love story in Book 4, Trusting Romance? Order it now!

If you want more romantic comedies, you can start with my Perfectly Imperfect Love Series. In Book 1, a photographer has to move in with a baseball player. And don't forget to grab your free copy of the Meet-Cute Mishap by joining my newsletter, plus receive freebies, giveaways, and so much more!

ABOUT THE AUTHOR

USA Today & International bestselling romance author, S.E. Rose lives near Washington D.C. with her family. When she's not wrangling her cats or keeping up with her kids, she's plotting her next story.

She loves all things wine, coffee, and cats. In her non-existent free time, she enjoys traveling, going to concerts, binging on her favorite shows, and reading, especially if it's a good mystery or comedy.

Learn more about upcoming books from S.E. Rose at www.seroseauthor.com.

ALSO BY S.E. ROSE

Deceitful Destiny Series
Island (Book 1)
Secrets (Book 2)
Bravura (Book 3)
Determination (Book 4)
Home (Book 5)

The Poisoned Pawn World
A Fierce Princess
A Valiant Prince
A Wise Prince
A True King
The Overnight Naughty List

The Kingmakers of Kensington
A Man of Power
A Man of Wealth
A Man of Prestige

Perfectly Imperfect Love Series

Undeniably Perfect
Hopelessly Perfect
Romantically Perfect
Awkwardly Perfect
Reluctantly Perfect

Brides of Banneker

Scoring the One
Landing the One
Fixing the One

Once Upon a Billionaire Rom-Com Series

The Billionaire and the Librarian
The Billionaire and the Maid
The Billionaire and the Runaway

Romances in the Building Series

Faking Romance (Book 1)
Finding Romance (Book 2)
Building Romance (Book 3)
Trusting Romance (Book 4)

Fanning the Flames Series (Co-authored with Sierra Hill)

Burned (Book 1)
Ignited (Book 2)
Scorched (Book 3)

Clearview Falls University Series (Co-authored with Sierra Hill)

Falling for the Fake Boyfriend (Book 1)
Falling for the Roommate (Book 2)
Falling for the Football Player (Book 3)
Falling for the Quarterback (Book 4)

Novels

Chronicles of a Hot Mess
Chronicles of a Rockin' Mess
The Decoy
Second Start (A Holiday Springs Resort Novel)
The Road Trip Romance

Novellas & Short Stories

Neighbor in Apartment No. 5
The Tinsel Tango
The Fighter
A Polar Pursuit (Vagabond Series)
A Forward Holiday
Love in an Elevator
When It Rains, It Pours
Misery Loves Company

Want to learn more? Visit www.seroseauthor.com.

www.ingramcontent.com/pod-product-compliance
Lightning Source LLC
Chambersburg PA
CBHW030137010826
48973CB00002B/606